THE UNTOLD TALE

To Walt Peih

Emil Sargent

THE UNTOLD TALE

Erik Christian Haugaard

Illustrated by Leo and Diane Dillon

HOUGHTON MIFFLIN COMPANY BOSTON

Other books by

Erik Christian Haugaard

Hakon of Rogen's Saga

A Slave's Tale

Orphans of the Wind

The Little Fishes

The Rider and His Horse

LIBRARY OF CONGRESS CATALOG CARD NUMBER 74-135133
ISBN 0-395-12366-6
PRINTED IN THE U.S.A.
SECOND PRINTING C

To Anna and Joseph Seld

CONTENTS

THE
UNTOLD
TALE

PROLOGUE

O<small>N</small> <small>THIS</small> <small>DAY</small> <small>OF</small> O<small>UR</small> L<small>ORD</small>, the twenty-fourth of February, sixteen hundred and forty-eight years since the birth of Our Blessed Saviour, has died at Frederiks Castle, our Sovereign, Christian the Fourth, King of Denmark and Norway. May God have mercy on his soul and give to him, in death, the peace which life withheld from him.

The King died at sunset. Now, as I write these words, the clock in the tower of the castle is striking midnight. The candle on my table is burning low, as is my life, for I have reached that age when thoughts and dreams turn to the past. To those who traveled beyond the borders of youth, the dead are sometimes more alive than the living.

Far have I risen since first my eyes saw the towers of Frederiks Castle and I was a youth of nineteen years. From begging my bread, I can now give sweet charity to others. From having not a door to close against the wind and the rain, I hold the keys to all the rooms of the castle. I am the King's Steward, the keeper of his accounts. Once long ago I dreamt of becoming more; but now as white hairs appear in my beard and multiply each year, as if they bred, I am satisfied and thank God for my good fortune.

Of the five children who were born to me, three God has spared, and so many grandchildren have I, that I have trouble remembering their names. To them, their grandfather is a stoutish man, who wears a black velvet doublet and a silver chain around his neck. I cannot tell them — for they would not understand — that inside that dignified old man lives still the child, who was born fifty-six years ago.

These last months, as my King and Master lay dying in the castle, I have thought of writing down on paper what my eyes have seen, before the Jester who comes to all — king and servant — shall make me blind. But I have feared that what I would tell, would only mirror my own or my Master's vanity. If I should describe the battle at Lutter am Barenberge, where Field Marshall Tilly defeated my Master, would I be honest? I was then paymaster to General Fuchs, and I was the youngest man in the army to hold such a position. Ay, there you are! Pride is already making me bray like a donkey. No, better to put away pen and ink, and use them only to write accounts, for numbers lie less than letters.

I hear the clock in the tower strike two, and as the candle on my table dies, I light a new one. The paper and ink are there in front of me, as are two newly cut goose feathers, never used and white as snow. The King

is dead, the castle is silent. Only the mice are about, why do I not go to bed?

Some say that dead men walk at night, when the moon has blanched the world. I have never seen a ghost; but that no man dies before memory of him among the living is utterly gone, I know to be true. A child I knew in my youth, thirty-seven years ago, still lives in my mind today, as if age and time did not exist. What if I told his story and not my own? But whose ears would his story please: that story which all men know, who have partaken in war, and yet none speak of? He was but waist-high and saw the world from that dwarflike height. Did he see more than the officer, from his proud post, sees, as he rides his steed across the battlefield?

The clock strikes three. The old King is dead: God give rest to his Soul. A week ago some musicians played their flutes for him, for he was fond of music; but he could no longer hear. May Angels play for him now.

I shall do it! I shall tell the story of the boy, for in the chronicle of his life lies the untold tale of my own. And if I do it with honesty and skill, then that poor little ghost, who has haunted me, shall haunt all men who seek command, and yet have within their breast, a heart inclined to pity.

May Christ His Blessing give to this work and let me live to finish it.

CHAPTER ONE

The Father

THE MAN WALKED with difficulty through the snow.
He was more tired than the snow was deep, and it was
long since he had eaten a meal. He stumbled, the toe
of his boot had caught in a root beneath the snow. He
cursed as he almost fell; then, regaining his balance, he
stood still and looked at the forest he was approaching.
Evening was near, and though it was April, the sky was
winter dark. Heavy snow clouds rising like mountains,
high into the sky, foretold of a coming storm.

The man swung his arms, hitting his back as hard
as he could, to get warmth; then he held his hands together and blew into them; finally, like a suckling child
he put his fingers in his mouth. A gust of wind blew into
his face and he grimaced. The wind still came from the
east as it had all winter. As if he had suddenly realized
the hopelessness of standing still, he started to walk
briskly. But he had not gone far when again he slowed
down and let his feet shuffle through the snow.

The man was of no importance, except to himself
and his family. He was a poor farmer who cultivated

a few acres of sandy soil on north Zeeland, rented from the Crown. The owner of the land, King Christian the Fourth, had never seen this man; but he often mentioned him and his likes — in conversations with his advisors and in his letters to foreign kings — when he spoke of his "people."

The man was on his way to the town of Elsinore in search of charity, for he and his family were starving. The harvest had been poor that year. The frost had come early and spoiled the autumn grazing. Had he slaughtered two of his cows in September, when the frost had first come, he might have saved the third. But he had tried to keep them all alive, and by New Year they were only skin and bone — and still he could not kill them. He had not acted any more wisely about the horses. He should have sold the older one while he still could. The mare died just before Christmas, and now the young gelding was so weak that it would be of little use to him, even if it did survive till spring.

He was a good man, a kind man, who willingly worked hard; but he trusted too much in God and too little in himself. A weak plank is of little consequence to a ship, as long as the sea is calm; but when the waves beat against the hull that board breaks, and the ship sinks.

Night had already come to the forest. The man paused before entering it and glanced back into the twilight of the fields. For a moment he thought of returning to the farm.

'I have started too late,' he thought. 'I shall not reach

Elsinore before the middle of the night and the gates will be closed. But if I go back now, I may be too weak to set out tomorrow. And there is no food at home.' He closed his eyes as he tried to reach a decision.

"Oh, Lord!" he muttered, "I am a luckless man." And he plunged into the forest.

In the beginning the snowflakes came down slowly, gently, one by one; but soon the storm was upon him. The wind used the forest as its lute; each tree and each branch were strings upon which to play. The night grew soft and white with the snow. He seemed to be able to see. He lifted his head, turned to look about him, and his face struck a branch. When he looked down again, the path had disappeared. As the storm made him blind, he bent his head forward and stretched out his arms in front of him, for he feared walking into a tree. Suddenly his foot slipped; he stumbled and fell. 'It's a fox hole,' he thought; and he lay there thinking that in such weather, in the forest a man was less than a fox.

Slowly he rose, lifted his hands to his mouth to warm them with his breath, and walked on. He trudged against the wind, knowing that it blew from the east and this was the direction of Elsinore. A curious calm overcame him, as if the very wildness of the weather, and the great struggle to make his way against the wind, left only enough strength within him for the simplest thoughts.

"I should have slaughtered two of the cows," he mumbled out loud, "and then sold the mare." He smiled

at his own folly, and felt comforted that the decisions he
had not been able to make when it mattered, he could
make now. "Ay, a fool I have been! A fool!" And
having confessed this truth, he felt wonderfully relieved,
and certain that he would reach Elsinore and obtain help.

All of a sudden it stopped snowing, but the wind kept
up its melancholy song. The storm was not yet over;
it had merely paused to gain strength. The clouds parted
and a few stars appeared; the split widened and the moon
came out. The man was grateful to be able to see about
him; but the wind seemed stronger, more like a knife.
To his right there was open land. He walked towards it,
hoping it was a tilled field and that he was out of the
forest.

It was a large, flat plain and all around there were
woods. He had taken only a few steps when he knew
where he was. It was Gurre Lake. He was still in the
forest and far from Elsinore.

He walked eastward along the shore. Gurre Lake was
not a place where anyone would wish to be, in the middle
of the night. 'I should have gone home. There is no
blessing in this night.' He thought of his wife and son,
and of what might become of them if he did not return
from Elsinore with food.

On the frozen lake something moved, a dark shadow.
What was it? The man stood still; a cloud obscured the
moon.

"Jesus Christ, My Saviour!" he muttered. "It is the
King!" With his foot he drew a cross in the snow to
protect him.

The man knew well the story told by the peasants who lived near Gurre Lake. It was said that evil King Valdemar could not rest in his grave, but rode at night through the forest of Gurre with his men and his dogs. The eyes of his horse were burning coals and fire came from its nostrils. King Valdemar had lived long ago, when there still had been monks at Esurm Cloister — his queen was buried there. Now the monks had been gone more than a hundred years, and King Christian had torn down their cloister to build Frederiks Castle; but still Valdemar could not rest in his grave like a good Christian.

'God is unforgiving,' he thought; then he said aloud, "Protect me, My Saviour, against trolls and witches and those who walk in the night."

The moon came out again and illuminated the frozen lake. The two deer saw the man and leapt for cover.

'If only I could have caught a deer!' the man thought. But the animals of the forest belonged to the King and only the King's men were allowed to hunt them. Many times that winter he had thought of poaching, but he was by nature law-abiding. Soon the snow began to fall again, and he forgot about the deer, in the weary work of plodding against the wind.

By the time he came to the other end of the lake and the ruins of the old castle that King Valdemar had built, he was too tired to go any further. He found shelter by one of the crumbled walls. 'It is a blessing to be out of the wind,' he thought; and he no longer felt so cold.

'I'll rest till morning,' he decided. 'There is no reason

to walk on, the gates of the city are closed.' He sat down and huddled against the wall, where the snow was so deep that it almost covered him.

Half in a dream, he saw himself coming home to his farm with food; he smiled and fell asleep. The snow fell all night, though just before dawn the wind stopped. By noon, the weather had changed. The sky was blue. The spring that he had been waiting for was finally about to come; but to the man it did not matter, for he had died in his sleep.

CHAPTER TWO

The Mother

THROUGH the small glass window, the only one in the room, the strong April sunlight entered; at the sight of it, the woman lying in the alcove bed smiled. She wanted to get up but she was too weak. She called for her husband; but then she remembered that he had set out for Elsinore, the day before, and could not be home before evening.

She thought of Elsinore. There she had been born and had lived until her marriage. She saw the streets and the houses. She did not see them as they were now with snow on their roofs, but as they were in summer with roses growing up against their walls. She smiled as she imagined herself walking along the beach, where the rowboats of the ferrymen were drawn up.

Her father had been a ferryman, one of those who made his living by rowing merchants and sailors out to the great ships that lay at anchor in the Sound. All the ships that passed through the Sound — that strait which connects the Baltic Sea with the Kattegat — had to stop at Elsinore to pay a tax to the King. Often the ships would tarry, for the roadstead at Elsinore was a safe place to weather a storm. Sometimes there would be as many as half a hundred ships riding at anchor; then the ferrymen's business went well, and you could hear them sing as they rowed. But in winter there were few ships; and the ferrymen and their families would often have to dream of their suppers instead of eating them.

When the woman had been a child, she had helped her father by hailing strangers who were heading towards the beach. She would ask them if they were in need of a ferryman; and if the answer was yes or a nod — and not a curse — she would lead them by the hand to her father's boat. Often she had been given a ginger cake or even a copper coin, for she had been fair as a child, and many a sailor looking into her blue eyes had been reminded of his own daughter or of a younger sister. When she had grown older, her father had forbidden her to speak with strangers; and her younger brother had been sent to fetch customers. This she had felt to be a great injustice.

She had loved the town: the gay, crowded streets and the foreign sailors, who spoke languages she could not understand. Once — the summer that she was ten — she had seen a sailor who had a monkey dressed in a red jacket sitting on his shoulder, and she had been allowed to pet the little creature.

She lifted her hand and frowned. Some slight noise in the room had disturbed her thoughts. As she had grown weak, her soul no longer seemed to be fettered to her body. It seemed free to leave, free to travel as her dreams desired. Often she had reasoned to herself that it had been only her body that her husband had brought to the lonely farm; but since the body is the house of the soul, her soul had come too: as a prisoner. Now as sickness and want made that house a ruin, her soul was free to roam. She did not realize that also this freedom was curtailed, nor did she wonder why it only led backwards, into her childhood.

As the woman slowly glided into the sleep of death, tomorrow disappeared and took with it today, leaving only yesterday as real. Her father had been dead ten years at Michaelmas, her mother four years at midsummer; and yet now they were more alive to her than her son, who sat at the table looking at his hands, as if they were a book and he could read.

The door to the stable had been left open; it swung on its leather hinges and banged against the wall. The noise could be heard in the house, but the woman in the alcove bed did not recognize it. Only yesterday, she would have called the boy and sent him outside to close it; a week ago, she would have gone herself. Now the banging door sounded to her like the noise that a loose stay makes, as it beats against the mast of a ship.

The boy got up and walked quietly to his mother's bed. He was their only child. God had given them no more, perhaps because three mouths were all such poor sandy soil could feed.

The woman recognized the boy and smiled, but the effort was so great that she closed her eyes again. The room disappeared and she was back in Elsinore, lying on her bed beside the alcove in which her parents and her younger brothers slept.

The home of her childhood had been small and humble. The little cottage had leaned against its neighbor, a larger house where a ship's carpenter lived; that, in turn, had a common wall with a bigger building until — as the final link in a chain — came the great house of a noble family whose name was Ox, and in whose hall the King often dined when he was in Elsinore. The whole town had been hers: the cloister that was now the House of the Poor; the great Church of Saint Olaf; yes, even the King's castle was part of her house, for her uncle was the cook in the commandant's kitchen.

Even in winter, when hunger had been a constant guest, it had not seemed so terrible, for the other ferrymen and their families had fared no better. "Good luck is not eternal," she had often heard them say, "but neither is its absence." They knew that the ice in the Sound must break up; the big ships would come, and the cry of a sailor for a ferryman would again be heard.

But the farm to which her husband had brought her stood by itself, ever so alone. In winter even the landscape was bare. The walls of the town kept nature out unless it was invited to enter as a rose or a cherry tree. When the wind blew through the streets of the town, it was an intruder, not a master, as it was when it danced with the sandy soil of King's Acre, pressing itself through the walls of the farm and depositing dirt everywhere.

The first winter she had told her husband that she

was frightened, and begged him to allow her to return to Elsinore. But he had not understood her fears and even less, her longings. To him the townspeople were a drunken, godless lot; no more honest than thieves. He would tell her about farmers who had gone to market with a cow and returned without a copper in their purse. She had thought of running away; and perhaps she would have, had the path to Elsinore not led through the great forest. The fourth summer of her marriage the boy had been born.

The child had brought back her laughter. At night, she would sing psalms to him; but sometimes, when her husband had gone to look after the cows, before he went to bed, she sang songs that she had heard the sailors sing. She had thought much about the boy, dreamed many a fair dream for him; but in none of them did he grow up to be a farmer.

The boy touched his mother's cheek. She opened her eyes and, for a moment, she was back on the farm. She looked at the child and with great difficulty said his name, "Dag."

The boy answered, "Mother . . ." and waited for her to say something to him; for he did not understand that she was dying, only that she was sick.

The mother said no more. She smiled and then closed her eyes again; but this time her soul did not travel to Elsinore, to see its towers and spires and lofty ships.

CHAPTER THREE

The Boy

THE BOY KNELT on the bench trying to look through the little window into the yard of the farm; but the glass was so poor that he could hardly see through it, and it acted as a mirror. The boy moved his face just slightly and now his reflection had four eyes. He smiled and cocked his head and he had two noses like a witch.

It was an old game and he soon grew tired of it. He climbed down from the bench. In a corner of the room, near the open fireplace, was a tiny shelf where his play-things were kept. He took down one of the flint stones that he had found the summer before, when he had gone with his father to gather seaweed at a beach. The sea had worn a hole through the stone. The boy stuck his little finger through the hole. He had eight such stones. They were different sizes, and each represented an animal. The two larger ones were a team of horses; the others were cows and sheep. When he played out of doors, he tied a string through the holes and tethered his animals in the field. Each of his stone animals had a name and he knew its particular nature. The largest stone was a stallion; it was willful, liable to break its tether and run away.

He heard the barn door bang; it must have blown open. He knew that he ought to go out and shut it. He put his stones away but he remained in the room. He was afraid to go out to the stable, for he had been there in the morning and found the gelding dead. Its eyes had been all white.

He walked back to the table and sat down on the bench. He looked at his hands and carefully counted his fingers, as if he expected to have lost one. He broke the silence of the room by whispering, "Mother . . ." But the dying woman in the bed alcove did not hear him. He said the word again, a little louder; then he rose and tiptoed to the bed.

He stood still gazing at his mother; she appeared so small, as if she were a child now, too. He touched her cheek gently. She seemed cold to his touch, and yet her forehead was bathed in sweat. Slowly his mother opened her eyes and whispered his name. He shouted: "Mother!" But she turned her head towards the wall.

Again he heard the banging of the door and this time he went out to close it.

He need not have looked inside. He could just have closed the door and let the wooden latch fall into place. But once he had looked, he had had to enter. The young horse was still lying where it had fallen, its neck outstretched; all the bones of its body were visible through its skin. He could hear the breathing of the two cows who were still alive, but he did not dare approach them. He looked about for something to feed them. There was nothing, not even a handful of chaff. He noticed the straw roof, and the idea occurred to him of tearing out some straw and giving it to the cows.

He climbed the ladder to the loft; it was empty, swept clean even of dust. With his hands, he tore at the roof. It was old and the straw crumbled into ragged bits. Carefully, he collected an armful, taking small amounts from several different places, in order not to destroy the roof.

He climbed down into the stable. Both the cows were lying down. The boy divided the straw and put a bundle next to each cow's head. Neither of them made any attempt to rise; they were too weak to take any interest in dry dust.

When he came outside, the boy looked up at the blue sky; spring really was on its way. The icicles still hung from the eaves; but the sun had gained strength enough to make its warmth felt. The boy broke off a long, pointed icicle and sucked on it. He had not eaten since the day before; his father had made a gruel of barley before he had left for Elsinore. Dag wondered whether there might be something left in the pot; and even though he knew there wasn't, he returned to the house to look.

The pot was empty; he had scraped it himself that morning. He put a few sticks on top of the ashes that hid the embers and blew until they caught fire. He emptied water from the earthen pitcher into the iron pot, and hung the pot on the hook above the fire; though there was no reason to boil water, for he had nothing with which to make either soup or gruel.

Thinking that his mother might want something to drink, he filled his father's tin cup with water. Her face was still turned towards the wall. He called to her and when she did not answer, he bent forward and touched her.

Her eyes told him that she was dead; they were like the cow's had been when she died: empty. He tried to put the cup down on the table carefully, but even though it was not filled to the brim, he spilled a little of the water. He dried it up with his sleeve. Tears ran from his eyes, but he cried soundlessly. Twice he called out: "Mother . . . Mother . . ." But in the tone of his voice there was neither expectancy nor hope. Then he screamed: "Father!" and ran out of the house pursued by his own fear.

He ran as quickly as he could past the two neighboring farms, that had been abandoned not long after New Year. When he reached the great forest, the sun was low on the horizon and the darkness of the woods frightened him. Reluctantly, he started back to the farm; but then he thought that he might have been wrong: that his mother might not be dead, and he started to run.

He entered the house out of breath. In the silence of the room, he could hear his own heart beating and he knew that he had not been mistaken. He did not walk to the alcove but to the fireplace. He looked into the iron pot; and since the water had boiled away, he filled

it. With great care he rebuilt the fire. He did everything slowly, wanting it to take time.

He sat by the fire all night, waiting and listening for
his father's footsteps. Once he heard an owl hooting.
The sound came down through the chimney into the
room; he closed his eyes and shuddered, although his
father had told him that it was not true that owls were
the souls of dead people.

When the first grey light of morning came, he fell
asleep on his little stool, his head resting in his hands.
He slept until the middle of the morning when melting
snow, falling from the roof into the yard, awakened him.

Without looking around the room, he hurried outside. The sun was so bright that it almost blinded him,
and the sky was clear. There were hardly any icicles
hanging from the eaves; the smashed bits of once
foot-long cones lay glistening on the ground. The boy
ran down to the pond; the ice was so soft that he was
able to make marks in it with a stick.

Suddenly, as he stared at the lines he had been draw-
ing in the ice, he felt certain that his father would not
come back. He started to cry. Where was he to go?
Who would help him? He looked over his shoulder
towards the house; a little smoke was coming from the
chimney. He had tried to pray during the night; but he
knew only two prayers: the one you said before going
to bed and the one of thanks recited before meals.

High above in the sky a lone swan was flying; Dag
heard the beat of the wings. He dried his eyes and raised
his head to look at it. "My father is dead," he said

aloud. Then it was that it occurred to him to go and tell the King what had happened. His father had rented his land from the Crown, but the King was far away. "He doesn't know that we're starving!" the boy almost shouted. He — Dag — would tell King Christian of their misery and the King would help him. By some kind of miracle, the King would set all things right again; his mother and father would be alive and the mare and the gelding and the cows would be well. Everything would be as it had been last summer — no! as it had been last spring, before the drought.

He ran back to the house to make himself ready for his journey. His first thought was to find something in which to carry his stones; then he decided to take only the best one, the stallion. A moment later he told himself that he was foolish, and he was so ashamed that he took all the stones and dumped them into the well.

He was wearing his warmest clothes and his boots. After finding his knitted cap, he looked around the room, though his glance carefully avoided the alcove bed. He wanted to take the large knife, but it had no sheath and he wondered how he could carry it. What he needed was a piece of rope, and when he found one, he tied it around his tunic and stuck the knife into it. His father's tin spoon fitted nicely beside the knife. He was determined to take the tin cup as well, but he did not want to carry it in his hand; finally, he shoved the cup inside his tunic. His father's staff — the one he used to drive the animals — stood by the door; the boy grabbed it and found that he was ready. He opened the door and

hesitated; but finally, he lifted his head and forced himself to glance at the alcove bed.

"I will come back, Mother," he called aloud. Then he
walked out into the sunlight and closed the door behind
him.

The boy stood in the middle of the farmyard holding
the staff, which was twice his height, in his hand. He
nodded to the house and to the barn, to say goodbye
to them. Feeling that the moment was solemn, he
dropped down on his knees in the wet snow and recited
the prayer that he usually said before he got into bed.
When he was almost finished, he remembered that he
was wearing his cap, and he took it off. He was seven
years old, Dag of King's Acre; and he was all alone.

A month later, the land was rented out again. A new
farmer arrived with horses and cows. The body of Dag's
mother was carried to the church at Gurre; and she was
buried in the eastern part of the churchyard near the
fence, farthest away from the church.

CHAPTER FOUR

In the Forest

KING'S ACRE was part of a large clearing and when Dag climbed the last stone fence, he was in the forest. To those who do not know the forest, it appears as pathless as the sea. If you cannot read the language of nature, and find your course by the angle a tree trunk makes with the earth, or the way the moss covers a stone, then you are liable to walk in circles.

Dag wandered deeper and deeper in the forest, though one could not say that he had lost his way, for he did not know where he was going. A breeze came and the clouds gathering in the west obscured the sun. He could not feel the wind; but the topmost branches of the trees sighed as it blew through them. He was troubled by the clouds, for they promised nothing pleasant to anyone caught out-of-doors.

The snow was wet and it caked under the wooden soles of his boots. He stopped several times to scrape it off. To still his hunger, he ate the little buds from the branches of a young tree.

At Christmas, when the Sound had first frozen, it had been said that packs of wolves had crossed the ice from the north. Now Dag remembered this and listened, expecting at any moment to hear the cry of a wolf. The boy startled a hare and it jumped out from its hiding place behind a bush. Dag started to run. He fell and the tin cup rolled out of his tunic. He picked it up, and walked on with his head bent down. He was not as afraid of falling, as he was of what he might see, if he held his head up. It was beginning to be twilight, and the boy had been told that in the darkness of the woods live all the shadows of the world. Only the night people, gypsies and poachers, dare be in the forest when night falls.

It was by chance that he found the little shelter. It had been built the autumn before by a hunter and was made of branches loosely woven together. Most of the leaves had long ago withered and fallen, so that the shelter could not give much protection against rain or snow; but it was a cage for Dag's courage. He closed the opening as well as he could with branches that he found nearby; then he placed his knife before it, for it is well-known that trolls do not like to step over steel. He made four little crosses of sticks, and placed them so that there was one pointing towards each of the four corners of the world; this he had seen his father do in the stable at King's Acre, to keep out ghosts.

Luckily, the weather really had changed and the night was not cold. Damp it was and the boy shivered; but his feet were warm. His boots were in good repair, though their last greasing had been in the fall, when there had been lard to spare for such things. Dag said his prayer out loud, but he was too frightened to lie down. In the stillness of the night his fears even forbade him to cry. The clock of terror runs slowly and it counts minutes as hours.

Suddenly the boy heard a noise more distinct than the other forest sounds. It was an animal approaching his tiny shelter. Dag thought it was a wolf and picked up his knife to defend himself. He wasn't as terrified as he had expected to be; fear, like hunger, wears out its sharpness if it lasts too long.

He had anticipated that the animal would break through the branches and attack him, but it sat on its haunches, waiting. He could hear from its breathing that it had run far; and he imagined the red tongue hanging out between the rows of white teeth. If it was a wolf, it was probably waiting for its pack; but why didn't it howl to call them? Now the boy heard another animal approaching. It was larger and walked as heavily as a wild boar.

"Satan," said a deep, low voice. "Satan?"

"Jesus Christ!" Dag whispered, and he would have added "protect me," but he could say no more; it was as if someone were holding onto his throat.

"What have you got there?" the man asked the dog and Satan whined in reply. Then the man shouted towards the little shelter, "Are you one of those who cannot be abroad after the red cock of morning crows?"

Dag did not answer, though he felt relieved that whoever was outside was not a ghost or the devil. "I am only a boy," he whispered at last.

The man laughed; and though Dag did not recognize it, there was relief in his laughter. "Come out," the man said, tearing apart the flimsy barrier that Dag had constructed.

In the darkness the man appeared larger than he was and Dag did not dare look up at him. Laughing more kindly than before, the stranger bent down and put his hand under the boy's chin.

"I am Lars. Some people call me Black Lars and use my name to frighten their children, but I have never done any child harm. What is your name?"

"Dag," the boy whispered.

"Dag . . . 'Day' . . ." the man repeated. "And why did they give you such a name?"

"I was born at Midsummer, just as the sun rose, and Maren Eriksdaughter who came to help my mother said it was a good omen and that I should be called Dag." The boy had heard the story of his birth told so often that he could repeat it now, although he was trembling with fear.

"I suppose you've heard what they tell of me," Lars said quietly. "They say that I am robber and that I have killed a man. But they are lying. I have stolen nothing, for the animals of the woods are wild things and belong to no one." This was an argument that Lars often used; but even though he had persuaded others that he was right, he remained unconvinced himself.

"My mother and father are dead!" the boy cried. Dag

had meant to say the words slowly, but he had blurted them out, and now he could not stop himself from crying.

The dog growled and Lars commanded it to be still. "So you are all alone?" he asked.

The boy sniffled so that he could speak; he was about to say something about being on his way to see the King, when he realized that it would not be wise to mention the King to a poacher. "Yes, I am alone," he whispered.

The dog snarled. Black Lars looked down at it, and then took a piece of dried deer meat from under his tunic, which he handed to the boy. At once the dog whined and wagged his tail. "You will give Satan the meat but only when I tell you to. Dogs are like women. If you treat them gently but make them obey you, they will lick your hands."

Suddenly hunger tore at Dag, as if an animal with sharp claws were living in his stomach. Only his fear of Black Lars kept him from eating the meat.

"Sit," the men commanded; and the dog sat on its haunches and raised its front paws as if they were hands. Dag had never seen a dog do this before. "Now hold up the meat," Lars ordered.

Dag stretched out his trembling arm and closed his eyes, expecting the dog to leap up and bite his hand.

"Now," said Lars.

Slowly the boy opened his eyes; it was a moment before he could make out the shape of the dog. There it was, waiting with its jaws open, and Dag dropped the meat between the two rows of sharp white teeth.

"Are you hungry?" Lars asked and Dag replied so emphatically that the man laughed. "You look as scared as a hare, but I think you eat meat."

He handed Dag a larger piece than he had given to the dog. Without knowing it, the boy moaned, then he tore at the meat ferociously. Lars turned away and an expression of pain passed over his face. When the boy had swallowed the last bite, he patted him on the head, almost in the same manner that he fondled the dog.

"Come," he said softly.

The boy had difficulty keeping up with Lars, who walked rapidly and did not even seem to notice that branches whipped against his face. They were in that part of the great forest that stretched from Frederiks Castle to the sea, where the oak tree predominated. Here the undergrowth was dense, for the oak is more generous than the beech tree and allows the sun's rays to pass through its branches. A twig had caught Dag's knitted cap and was difficult to remove without tearing the yarn. He called out for Lars to wait. The poacher turned around; at first he looked annoyed but then he smiled.

It was almost dawn when they came to the hillock. The dog had run ahead and was waiting patiently for them at the base of the mound. The poacher carefully lifted an armful of branches, revealing a hole that looked like the entrance to a giant fox burrow. Satan immediately disappeared into it and with a nod, Black Lars motioned for the boy to follow.

Dag hesitated; the hole was frightening. He looked

up at the poacher and Black Lars smiled reassuringly. "Crawl in and be welcome in my house."

Slowly, on all fours as if he, too, were a dog, Dag made his way into the earth, into the darkness.

CHAPTER FIVE

In the Grave Chamber

THE TUNNEL was not long and led into a small stone chamber. In the dim light from a tallow candle and the charcoal fire, Dag made out the great boulders which were the walls. He heard a whimper and turned to see a woman, sitting on a bed of skins with a baby in her arms. He bowed towards her, as his mother had taught him to do, when he was introduced to strangers.

The woman laughed. "What have you caught, Lars? Is it a hare?" The man grunted and went to the fire to look into the pot. "Haven't you got enough mouths to feed, that you have to bring home another?" The woman spoke loudly. She lifted the child to her breast. Greedily, the little one continued the meal which the arrival of Dag and the poacher had interrupted. "You look hungry," she shrieked at Dag. "Would you like to suckle too?" She bared her other breast.

The boy, who had been slowly retreating from her, bumped the back of his head against the stone wall. The woman laughed and covered her breast.

Lars had taken off his sheepskin coat and was warming his hands at the fire. "I found him in the forest," he said quietly.

"Why didn't you leave him there? The wolves have to eat too — not that he would make much of a meal, not even for a wolf."

"Mind your tongue, or I'll feed both you and your girl to the wolves," Lars replied gruffly.

Dag glanced from one to the other, unbelievingly. His own parents, when they were angry, had always been silent; and he had been taught that angry words were like curses.

Pointing at the woman, Black Lars shouted, "But maybe the wolves wouldn't want to eat a witch!"

Dag was startled by the word "witch." He had heard about a witch who had poisoned all the cows in Esrum. He looked at the woman fearfully. She was not old and her nose was small. 'She is probably one of the night people,' he thought, 'a gypsy, for her hair is black.' Dag had seen a gypsy once; his father had sold some skins to him. He had worn a gold ring in one of his ears.

Noticing that the boy was staring at her, the woman grinned. "Shall I change you into a toad, my little friend?"

"No . . . No, Ma'm," he replied and again bowed in her direction.

This delighted the woman. "No, not a toad. I shall change you into a fawn and keep you for myself and put a bell around your neck."

"Be careful," Lars said to the woman, "or I'll change *you* into something."

Black Lars's threat did not seem to frighten her. She put the baby down slowly and covered it carefully, before she took the few steps to the fire. She stirred the stew and brought the ladle to her lips. She sniffed at it and blew on it. She seemed satisfied with what she had tasted. Lifting the heavy iron pot from the hook above the fire, she placed it on the floor in front of the bed of skins.

"In God's name," she said.

Lars was half reclining on the furs. In his hand, he was holding two spoons: one made of wood and the other of horn. He gave the wooden spoon to the woman, and she sat down beside him. Without saying a word to the boy, they both began to eat.

Dag drew nearer and nearer; at last, he knelt down, on the other side of the pot.

"We have only two spoons," the woman said. "You'll have to wait till one of us is finished. If there's any left . . ."

From his belt, Dag drew out his tin spoon. The woman grabbed it and gave it to Black Lars. The poacher was about to give Dag his horn spoon, when he changed his mind and handed it to the woman. Finally, the boy was offered the wooden spoon. He took it without complaining, for he knew that the switching of the spoons gave him a right to eat.

The food tasted good. It was cabbage mixed with deer meat. Fearing that the pot would soon be empty, the boy ate as fast as he could, without giving himself time to chew the meat. But the pot had been well filled.

There was easily enough for three. It was the first time in more than a month that Dag had eaten heartily.

When the pot was empty, he licked the wooden spoon carefully as he had been taught to do; then he stuck it in his belt, indicating by this act Black Lars's right to the tin one.

"Do you know where you are?" The man stretched out on the skins. "It's a grave chamber." Lars looked proudly around the dark, dungeon-like room. "It's the grave chamber of a king."

The word "king" made the room seem different to the boy and he examined it once more. Although it was not very large, the stones of which it had been built were huge. It was low and a grown man could not stand upright in it. The fire burned in a niche that had been made by removing one of the smallest of the stones. The absence of smoke in the room told that above that recess, there must be a hole through which it could escape.

"What king?" Dag asked. It had never occurred to him that, just as there had been farmers who had rented King's Acre before his father, there had also been many kings of Denmark.

"In the very old times . . ." Black Lars paused, to try to think of a way of explaining to the boy, how long ago he meant. "Long, long ago . . . before Christ Our Saviour walked this earth, there lived giants here in the north and this is the grave of a giant king."

"It's all lies!" the woman exclaimed. She was pouring water from a wooden bucket into the iron pot.

"This is the home of his parents. He was born here. His mother had horns on her head and a long tail trailing behind her."

"Ay." Black Lars laughed. "But I married beneath me. For a proper troll, to marry a slut like you, would be as bad as mating Satan, here, with a cur from the streets of Elsinore."

When he heard his name, the dog raised his head; but the man paid no attention to him, so the animal closed his eyes again and went back to sleep.

"Marry me, you did!" she said shrilly. "But I get as much good out of that, as the miller's horse gets from being married to the treadmill."

The arguments were not new. Time had dulled, not sharpened them, till they were the only language of love that the poacher and his wife knew.

"Bring me the jug," Lars ordered. The woman neither answered nor obeyed.

In the corner furthest from the fireplace, there were some bird nets and a stack of traps for catching hares; beside them was a stoneware jug. Lars, as he returned with it to the bed, slapped the woman on her behind. To the boy's surprise she only laughed.

Lars shook the jug. It was almost full. He yanked out the stopper and pressed the opening to his lips. When he finished drinking, he wiped his mouth with the back of his hand, and offered the jug to the boy. Dag knew from the smell that it was schnapps. His mother had given it to him once, when he could not sleep from the pain of a stomachache. He had not liked the way it had burned his mouth and throat, but he dared not refuse the poacher. With difficulty he lifted the jug to his mouth. He swallowed more than he had intended, and he began to choke.

Black Lars grabbed the jug for fear the boy might drop it; then he laughed. "It's like fire. The very best schnapps to be bought anywhere in Elsinore."

The boy's eyes were watering.

"Let the child be," the woman said. "Better to have left him to the wolves than to make a drunkard out of him."

Far away, Dag heard Black Lars laugh; then he felt himself being lifted up and carried to the bed. The skins were soft and warm.

CHAPTER SIX

The Poacher's Family

At first Dag did not know where he was, for he had dreamt that he was back on his father's farm. In his dream both his parents had been alive, and he had heard his mother sing. He looked in vain for the little window above the table. Then he remembered what had happened. He closed his eyes and tried to bring back the dream. But as anyone who has ridden a nightmare knows full well, we are not masters of our dreams; they carry no saddle and wear no bridle.

"Little hare," the woman said, "have you slept well, or did you dream of the fox or the wolf? You fell asleep so fast, you forgot to say your prayers."

Dag flung aside the skins and sat up. He had no idea how long he had slept, for inside the stone chamber it was always night. "Where is Lars?" he asked anxiously.

"What do you want him for? Aren't you afraid he might eat you or feed you to his dog?"

Dag shook his head, for he was not afraid of Black Lars anymore. "He's never killed anybody and he's never stolen anything. The animals . . . the animals of the woods are wild things and don't belong to anyone."

The woman laughed. "He should have left you to the wolves. Now he will have to carry you on his back for the rest of his life," she added seriously.

Dag looked at her wonderingly.

"If Black Lars had left you out there — as any sensible man would have — the only trouble you'd ever have been to him would have been the thought of what a short-eared hare could have been doing in the woods alone. But now that he's taken you in, he's responsible to God for you."

"Responsible to God?" Dag asked incredulously.

"If your father gave you a puppy and said it was yours, he'd want you to take care of it, wouldn't he?"

"Yes, Ma'm."

"Well, you're like a puppy. And one day God is going to ask Black Lars what he did with you. But Black Lars cannot say to God that you were just a lot of trouble, so he drowned you as he would have a puppy; because if he said that, then God would be certain to ask him why he hadn't left you to your fate, if he hadn't meant to take care of you. And that question Black Lars won't be able to answer, and he knows it. You're not like a bur that has gotten caught in his hair. He cannot just pull you out and throw you away." Abruptly, the woman turned away from Dag, as if at that moment she realized that he was merely a boy, and could not understand her. But still her thoughts demanded to be said aloud, so she added sharply: "You're lucky it wasn't me that found you, for I would have left you there where you were. My advice always is: never be anybody else's good luck, or they'll tie your arms behind you with their gratitude."

Dag said nothing. The tears were running down his cheeks; and he was glad that it was dark in the stone chamber, so that the woman could not see that he was crying. Suddenly he remembered that the night before, he had wrapped his father's tin cup inside his knitted cap, and placed it among the nets in the corner. He waited until the woman was absorbed in tending the fire; then he went in search of it.

He found the cap on the floor next to the stack of traps; the tin cup was not in it. In the dim light he looked about furtively; with his hands he probed among the nets, and then under the skins of the bed, coming as close to the sleeping baby as he dared.

It was nowhere to be found. He lay still on the bed and watched the woman move about the room. His anger grew, as he noticed with what sureness and ease she did her tasks in the darkened chamber. 'You're a thief!' he thought. 'You're a thief!'

Dag heard the branches rustle. Someone was coming. He leapt to his feet. He thought it was Black Lars and expected to hear Satan whimper. 'I'll tell him,' he thought; 'I'll tell him that she's taken my tin cup.'

A little man came crawling out of the tunnel, who was only a head taller than Dag and could easily stand upright in the grave chamber. He smiled a toothless smile towards the woman; but she did not seem pleased by her visitor, for she scowled and said nothing.

The man took off his cap and bowed towards Dag, as
if the boy were a mighty lord. His hair was long and
white. "God's blessing on you, young man. Have you
a copper to spare for an unfortunate old man who is
starving?" His pale blue eyes shot a quick glance towards the woman. "Ay, starving, though his own
daughter is as fat, and eats as well as any rich peasant
does! The world must prepare itself for the Second
Coming, when children forget God's Commandments,
and let their own fathers starve and thirst."

The woman started to lift the iron pot from the hook
and he reached under his sheepskin coat to take out
his wooden spoon. As she shoved the pot towards
him, he sniffed and then he wrinkled his nose.

"It's barley porridge with a little fat in it." Then
she added sternly, "Let the boy have some."

Dag looked up at her bewildered, but he drew the
spoon out of his belt and sat down next to the old man.
Every time Dag scooped a lump of the stiff porridge
onto his spoon, the old man pushed his arm and the food
fell back into the pot.

"Let him eat!" the woman commanded. "Or I'll take
a stick to you."

The old man ate so quickly that Dag only got a few
mouthfuls; but he was not very hungry because he had
eaten so well the night before.

"What's new at Frederiks Castle?" the woman asked.
"Is the King there?"

The boy sat bolt upright, and looked with wonder at
the man who might know where the King was.

The old man kept licking his spoon as if he had heard nothing. Finally, in a hoarse, rasping whisper, he muttered, "I'm dying of thirst."

The boy laughed as the old man twisted his mouth, shook his head, and groaned. The woman poured a little schnapps into a cup and gave it to her father.

He raised the cup towards her, as if he were about to make a toast before he drank. When he had finished drinking, he smacked his lips. "Aqua Vitae, the water of life, straight from the springs of Paradise."

"Paradise!" The woman laughed loudly, and Dag noticed that her teeth were white and straight. "Nay, Father, it is from another place. It is what the devil started his fires with, and no doubt you will get plenty of it, once you are dead."

Dag gazed at the old man thoughtfully and wondered how he could be her father, when she was a head taller than he was.

"Master Urbanius, who is a scrivener for the King and is fond of hares when they are well prepared . . ." He interrupted himself to wink at his daughter. "Master Urbanius claims that in heaven the angels wash themselves in Frankish wine. I doubt that, for I think no one washes in heaven because there, there is no opportunity to get dirty."

"You stink like a goat!" the woman said sourly.

Again, the old man pretended not to have heard her. "These are grave problems, my daughter, and they say that even the King cannot find answers to them, and he has asked the Bishop of Copenhagen . . ." Now he lowered his voice. "But if we were talking about smell, then I must tell what I have heard from the lying mouth of Ole Peg-leg, whose son is a gamekeeper. He talked about the smell of fox in the forest being too strong." He smiled merrily as if he were the bearer of good news.

The woman frowned and bit her lip. "There has been such talk before."

"True . . . true," he agreed pleasantly. " 'The dog is old,' said the fox as he climbed into the chicken coop, without giving a thought to the puppies who had grown . . .' There is a new gamekeeper from Jutland, way up there in the north, where the people are hardly Christian and they eat raw meat. The new gamekeeper has sworn that he will bring Black Lars to Frederiks Castle with a rope around his neck.

The baby was whimpering. The woman bent down and picked her daughter up and suckled her.

"He is a fierce dog," the old man continued. "He is fierce as a wolf, and so proud that he will kiss no hand but the King's. I have not been close enough to smell him; but I have seen him ride by on his horse, and he sits up so straight, you would think he was practicing to be captain of the guard."

"If he expects to catch every man who has caught a hare in the forest this winter, there will be no farmers to till the fields come spring," the woman said.

"True," her father agreed heartily. "It is as easy for the rich to be honest, as it is for the poor to be hungry. But it is Black Lars that he wants to catch. He is willing to pay five silver marks, to find out where his hiding place is."

"Five silver marks!" The woman was astonished.

Her father winked and grinned. "You could come and keep house for me. I should like to have a grand-daughter to bounce on my knee."

The woman laughed; and to Dag's amazement, spoke to him. "My father wants me to betray my husband for five silver marks. What do you think of that?" Then the expression on her face became one of fury and she shrieked at her father, "Had you lived in the time of Our Lord, you would have been Judas for a jug of schnapps and saved the Romans their silver!"

"My boy," the old man said to Dag, just above a whisper, "do you know what she's talking about? I have just asked my daughter, to come and live with her poor old father, instead of keeping company with a well-known criminal, to her everlasting shame."

There was a whistle. Father and daughter exchanged glances. "It's my husband," she said. "You must tell him of your plans."

Satan bared his teeth and growled as he entered. Black Lars grinned, "Well, Niels Goat, what brings you here?"

The dog walked up to Dag, sniffed at him, and lay down at his feet. The boy, who was very pleased by the dog's attention, bent down to scratch the animal behind the ears. "He thinks you're a puppy . . ." Black Lars said good-naturedly.

"If it please you," Niels Goat rose and bowed to the poacher, "I have news from Frederiks Castle."

Black Lars flung down the hare that he had been carrying. "Any news you bring is as welcome to me as a pair of fingernails are to a flea."

But when the woman repeated what her father had told her about the reward, the poacher listened carefully. "Five silver marks, that's a real sum," he said proudly.

Dag was staring at the poacher and wondering why he showed no fear. The boy knew that if Black Lars were caught, he was certain to be hanged. Dag remembered what his mother had told him, that those who were hanged could not be buried in Christian soil; and that their ghosts must walk abroad in the night until Doomsday.

"What has kept you from telling the King's dogs where to find me? I would as soon believe that you had turned honest, as that the hangman's noose is the gate to Paradise," Black Lars grumbled.

"Why should I bring misery to my daughter and my grandchild? I am as honest as any man."

"True, you are as honest as most men are, and that is why the world is filled with scoundrels!"

"I have been to matins, these last two Sundays," Niels Goat said. He glanced at his daughter to see whether this made any impression upon her.

"If the minister closed his eyes while he prayed, then I hope he counted the candlesticks afterward," she said and laughed.

The poacher laughed uproariously and slapped Dag

on the shoulder. If Niels Goat was angry, he hid it well, for he, too, joined in the merriment.

Black Lars was the first to stop laughing. Dag had not laughed at all, but had glanced with confusion from one grown-up face to the other. The poacher looked thoughtfully at his wife, as if he were asking himself a question and were in doubt about the answer.

Dag recognized the expression on Lars's face: sad and serious, but with more love than anger in it; thus the boy's father had looked at him during this long winter, but his father's pensive expressions had often been followed by sighs and sometimes by tears.

"Pain is short and joy is long. Where is the jug?" Black Lars was laughing again, though his laughter was not as gay as it had been. This a grownup, if his ears had been well cleaned by experience, would have recognized; but Dag could not, being yet too young to know the pain that comes from living.

The woman handed her husband the jug; at the same time she said to Dag, "You go outside; but stay by the hill; the forest is filled with wolves who like to eat little boys."

Dag wanted to remain. He turned to Black Lars, hoping that the poacher would ask him to stay.

"If you hear the bark of a dog, or see anything . . . anything but deer or wolves, give warning." Dag was hurt, not only because he had been sent away — for this his parents had done when they had something to discuss, which was not suitable for the ears of a little pitcher — but he was disappointed that Black Lars had repeated his wife's joke about wolves. While he was crawling through the tunnel, he decided that he would stay outside a long time — maybe all day.

Out in the sunlight, he squinted and stretched himself; then he realized with astonishment that it was late afternoon and that he had slept most of the day. Though the earth in many places was still snow-covered, the signs of spring were all around him. The branches were heavy with the buds of coming greenery; and near the trunks of many of the trees, where the snow had melted, the grass was green. The sky was almost summer blue; a few soft, fleecy clouds drifted across it. The beauty of autumn makes you reflect upon life, and your soul turns inward, making the call of the church bells for prayers not go unheeded; but spring is the time of dreams, when even the hopes of the most wretched will sprout and shoot green leaves.

Dag climbed to the top of the hillock. On the way he found the hole where the smoke came out. He peered into it. He could hear Black Lars's voice; but he could not understand what he was saying. The smoke smarted his eyes and he drew his face away.

On top of the hill was a big stone. It had been snow-covered only the day before, but now the snow had melted and it was dry. Dag sat down and scraped the snow from the soles of his boots. He wondered whether it was true, that this was the burial chamber of a giant king. It could just as well be the house of a troll.

He swung his feet up and pulled off his boots. He

noticed that there was a hole in one of his socks. Before
he removed them, he looked about, as if he feared that
someone might scold him. His feet were winter white.
He wiggled his toes and smiled; soon he would be able
to go barefoot again. Suddenly he thought of his mother;
perhaps the socks had reminded him of her, for she had
knitted them.

"Mother," he said softly, but to his surprise no tears
came. A feeling of shame came over the boy.

His thoughts turned to Black Lars. "He won't send
me away, his wife said he couldn't," he muttered as he
put his socks and boots back on. But as Black Lars's
wife came into his mind, he began to cry for he thought
once more of his mother.

When the cold breeze of evening began to blow, Dag
rose. He recalled that the poacher had told him to listen
for the sound of barking dogs. He stood still; all he
could hear was the wind in the trees. 'Lars is right,' he
thought. 'This is the grave of a king.'

As he bent down to pick up the branches that covered
the hole of the entrance, he heard singing. The singer's
voice was hoarse. Dag crawled through the tunnel and
saw Niels Goat dancing as he sang:

> *Drink, drink while you are able,*
> *Lift your glass and pour it down.*
> *Kings in ermelin and sable,*
> *The peasant in his woolen gown,*
> *Hate and curse the empty glass.*
> *Death will soon cut short our day,*
> *Therefore, let the bottle pass*

And our hearts be gay.
Hey for the glass, and hey for the wine,
And hey for the wench that is mine.

As the old man shouted the final line he tried to grab his daughter around the waist, and make her dance with him. But she stepped aside. He lurched and fell on the stone floor.

He lay motionless, while Black Lars and his wife exchanged glances.

"If his heart is still forever," said the woman, "then go and throw him in Esrum Lake, and let the fishes eat him."

Black Lars placed the side of his own face down flat on his father-in-law's chest, then he laughed. "The lake is frozen five feet down and I doubt if even the fishes would want his carcass." He picked the old man up in his arms and threw him on the bed of skins. "Besides, the day your father dies, you will know it by the smell of brimstone; the Long-tailed One, himself, is sure to come and get him."

"May it be soon," the woman muttered with hatred.

Dag, who was still crouching at the entrance of the grave chamber, made a slight noise. Black Lars looked down at him, and grinned at the frightened expression on the boy's face.

"If only King Christian would get into a blessed war with the King of Sweden, I could be a soldier. None would ask where I came from, once they'd seen me fire a musket. War is a good Christian thing. It can

make an honest man of an outlaw and spare the hangman work."

Black Lars was drunk; and though only Dag appeared
to be listening, he talked on and on. "Now what is an
outlaw but a poor man? And what is a thief but one
that needs to steal, for want of being able to fill his
stomach honestly? Would I live in the forest like a wild
animal if I had a farm of my own?"

Although the boy knew that he need not answer, he
said, "But my father had a farm and this winter we
starved."

"True, and your father isn't the only farmer who
died this winter. No one is invited to a funeral feast
because a sparrow dies." The poacher wrinkled his
brow, as if some thought persisted in eluding him. He
picked up the jug, shook it, and satisfied that it was not
empty, passed it to the boy.

The woman, who was stirring something in the big
iron pot, while she held the whimpering baby over her
shoulder, suddenly turned around and scowled.

"Schnapps is as good as Frankish wine," Black Lars
said.

"The Franks make wine from grapes, not barley," she
replied wearily.

Dag would have liked to insist that he had often heard
his father call schnapps wine; but all he had the courage
to do, to show his comradeship with the poacher, was to
take a large draught from the jug, which soon made him
so sleepy, that he could not follow the tale Black Lars
had begun to tell him.

What the man was recounting was the story of his life; and he was halfway through before he realized that Dag was asleep. The boy was lying across the bed. The poacher lifted him up gently and laid him next to the wall; then he covered him with a large skin.

The woman laughed and said that when he could no longer hunt, he could become a wet nurse. The poacher was not angry. He could not explain why, but the boy was to him like the dog, and he cared for them both. He reached out to scratch Satan behind the ears; the animal opened one eye to acknowledge the caress.

CHAPTER SEVEN

The Poacher's Story

No MAN has ever lived whose life has not been worthy of a story; yet the king and the poorest peasant often go to the same silent grave. And the marble tomb tells no more about the king, than the wooden cross, that marks the peasant's grave, tells about the man who rests beneath it.

The liquor which had loosened Black Lars's tongue had closed Dag's ears; this is an irony as age-old and common as the drunkard's tears. What was Lars's story? Why did he want to tell it to the boy? As man needs to wash and cleanse his body, so does he at times need to cleanse his soul. He needs to tell his secrets so that they will be secrets no longer; he needs to recapture his sorrows, so they will be lighter and easier to bear. If he could use the moon as an audience, he would, and howl at it, as dogs do when it is full; but man is not a dog — though he may sometimes bite like one — and only the ear of another human being can bring him comfort.

Lars had been born humbler than Our Lord Jesus, who had had a stable for a house and a manger for a bed.

The poacher's birthplace had been that great palace, whose roof is studded with stars and whose walls span all the beauty we know of. His mother had been a serving girl, who had herself known neither father nor mother. Being of a sweet and childish nature, she had been easily seduced by a fellow servant.

It is a common story; and yet that does not make it less pitiful. When she discovered that she was with child, she told her lover and he promised to marry her; but he bade her keep their coming union a secret. At Michaelmas, he disappeared. Some say that he became a soldier; others that he had taken berth on a merchant ship. Lars's mother had been abandoned; and now she must give birth to a child out of wedlock, for which crime the doors of the workhouse opened. Enlarging her skirts at night, when no one could see her sewing, she kept her secret.

When she felt that her time had come, she left the farm where she was a kitchen maid, and fled to the woods near Gurre.

Lars was born beneath an oak tree, in a small clearing in the forest. The frightened woman had planned to leave her child for the wolves to find; but when she held her naked babe in her arms, she decided it would be more merciful to drown it in Gurre Lake. She dragged herself to the water's brink. The lake was still. She began to tremble violently; then tearfully she prayed for her soul's salvation.

What was she to do? She could not return to the farm with her child; the baby would be taken from her and

she would have to stand trial. Near the outskirts of the
forest, there was a woodcutter's cottage. She placed her
baby in front of the door and fled.

As I have said, it is not an unusual story. The young
mother made her way through the forest to Elsinore,
where she found work. Later, she married. She had
known but fourteen summers when she had given birth
to Lars.

All that the poacher knew about his own origin was
that he was a foundling; this his foster mother had told
often enough. By chance, I learned the story of his
birth from the lips of his own mother, when I was a
lodger in her house in Elsinore. She was then an elderly
woman, a widow; and all her children were grown. I
was the first—and I believe the last—person to whom
she told her secret. She related her story as we sat by
the fire in her kitchen. When she had finished, she said,
"Sometimes, sir, I dream of him; and he is still a babe.
All the others are grown and I seldom see any of them,
for there isn't one who lives in Elsinore. Sometimes I
think about him, and I imagine that he has become a
great man. He — because I lost him — is more my own
than any of the others."

I asked her why, once she was married, she had not
tried to get her son back. She smiled and shook her head.
"Once, I walked so far that I could see the cottage, so
much did I long for my babe. But then I grew fearful
that I might be doing a great wrong. My good husband
was kind to his own children, but how did I know,

how he would treat *him?* And now, sire, if you were to
tell me what happened to my son, I should not think
kindly of you for doing it; for you would be taking him
from me, and I should be even more alone."

I said nothing, for if I had told her that I had known
her son, I should also have had to tell her that she had
chosen ill, when she had laid the babe before the house
of the woodcutter. Within there had lived a shrew with
a withered heart and her weak drunkard of a husband.
The couple had been childless and the boy should have
been a blessing, had there been any love within those
walls.

Lars's foster father did care for the boy. He taught
him how to set snares for the hare and how to make a
willow flute. But schnapps, the burning wine, was the
only master of the woodcutter's soul.

Lars's foster mother had been born with so many
curses within her, that a lifetime was not long enough to
shout them all. Nothing could make her happy or content. If Lars behaved, she called him an artful child who
was full of deceit. If he was naughty, she warned him
that he would grow up to feed the gallows. She was
even suspicious of Mother Nature. If it rained, she
would curse because she wanted to do her washing that
day. But if the heavens cleared, it would be either too
late or too soon to suit her. She thought her fellow
human beings were all scoundrels at best; and her tongue,
like a gale in winter, lashed at them from morning till
night.

When Lars was nine years old, his foster father died

and his foster mother had to leave the cottage. Work
was found for Lars on a nearby farm. There he spent
the next five years of his life, working from sunup till
sundown, for his board and his lodging, and the castoff
clothing of the farmer's sons. He was content during
those five years. For the first itme, he experienced the
luxury of a filled stomach; and he received no more beatings than the farmer's own children. The Christmas that
he was twelve, the farmer's wife presented him with a
scarf which she had knitted for him. He prized this gift
more than all the other things he possessed; even more
than the wild boar's tooth, he had found in the forest.
The minister had taught him to read; and at fourteen,
he was confirmed in the church at Gurre.

Now Lars was considered a grownup and he went to
work on an estate which belonged to the King. From
a silent child, shy of others, he grew into a man who
kept his own counsel, and whom his superiors regarded
as a person to be relied upon. Although he drank, he
was seldom drunk. He had a fondness for children and
animals. All should have gone well for Lars, had there
been any justice in this world; but to cry for justice is
like whistling in a storm. Luck, both good and bad,
seems to rule our lives.

When Lars was twenty, a new overseer came. He
was the son of a rich peasant; and the smell of the pigsty
was still about him, although he thought himself a nobleman. For no apparent reason, he took a dislike to Lars.
No, that is not true; no one dislikes another man without
reason. The new overseer had very good grounds for

hating Lars. He disliked the young man's free and open manner, and felt envious of the respect which the other workers showed him.

Lars had been a favorite of the former overseer, a man who knew that a good worker deserved to be trusted. Yet Lars had accepted the change meekly, for if nothing else, his foster mother had taught him —although it had been unwittingly — that hatred and resentment can drive both happiness and virtue away. Unfortunately, the overseer mistook Lars's resignation for weakness, and taunted him whenever they met.

It was during this time that Lars fell in love with Inger Nielsdaughter; and thus acquired Niels Goat as a father-in-law. Niels was a man to whom the word honesty had no meaning. Twice he had witnessed at witch trials, and had been paid well for his services. Although he was not respected by honest folk, he was like Master Diderik, the executioner at Elsinore, much feared. None but the worst ruffians ever came to his cottage; and Inger, who was motherless, had had a very lonely childhood. She had been seventeen when Lars had met her. Two weeks after he first set eyes on her, Niels Goat collected four witnesses; and Lars swore, in their presence, that he would marry Inger. This had been an act of foolishness; for Lars was both handsome and strong, besides being known as a good worker. There were more than a few men with farms of their own, who might have acquiesced to the pleading of a lovesick daughter and let him become their son-in-law. Inger's loneliness had attracted Lars: her loneliness which had seemed like his own. They had been married in spring; and before summer was over, Lars was an outlaw.

Evil to Niels Goat seemed part of his nature, just as goodness is part of that of a truly virtuous man. When sparks began to fly between the overseer and Lars, Niels blew on them to start a fire. At Midsummer, Saint Hans' Eve, when the young dance and feast the whole night through, Lars and the overseer got into an argument. Both were drunk, yet nothing would have happened, had Niels not egged them on. Prancing like a goat, the little man went from one to the other, repeating what Lars or the overseer had said; but he changed a word here and there, to make an insult deeper and the barbs more painful.

There was a fight and Lars won it. But it would have been better for him had he lost. The overseer's arm was broken; and he complained to the keeper of the castle, whose duty it was to make charges against Lars. When his arrest was ordered, he fled with his wife to the forest, to live as hunted as the deer.

This is what I can tell about Lars's life, up to that point, where Dag came into it. But how would Lars have told his own story, had the boy not fallen asleep? He would have told the tale differently, I am sure of that, and there would have been more truth in it — if truth is to be found in the heart of a man, in poetry. But Dag slept and Lars had to keep his sorrow within him. He started to blow softly on his little willow flute. The melancholy music woke his wife. She lifted her head, saw him sitting hunched before the fire, and called him to come to bed.

CHAPTER EIGHT

Alone Again

NAUGHT WILL HAPPEN to you or your child; I told you, it is Lars he is after," Niels Goat whispered hoarsely. He was sitting by the fire eating; and his daughter was standing beside him.

Dag opened his eyes but he did not move. The light from the fire was shining on Niels's face; and Dag noticed the bump on his forehead, from his fall the night before. A little gruel ran from the corner of his mouth, down into his beard. Near Dag the poacher was still sleeping and the boy could hear his deep breathing.

"He," and Niels gestured towards the bed, "is only a flea and the nails of the King are ready to crush him." Niels held up his hand and brought the long dirty finger-nails of his thumb and one of his fingers together.

"As for fleas, dear father," the woman said in a normal tone, "you know more about them than most men, since you keep a kingdom of them. But I think it will end in scratching and nothing more."

"Scratching, huh!" Niels looked with disgust at his daughter, as he licked his spoon. " I tell you that the noose for his neck has already been knotted," he whispered.

The woman turned to look at her husband; and Dag closed his eyes, though she could not have seen whether he had them open or shut.

"I have a plan," Niels whispered. "Come outside and I'll tell you everything."

The woman laughed scornfully, yet her curiosity was so great that she agreed. "If you are ready to leave now, then I'll walk with you as far as the great oak."

The old man leapt to his feet; he was grinning broadly. Yet even Dag, who did not like the woman, did not believe that she would betray her husband. Here lay the reason, why so many of Niels' plans were failures. He did not realize that all men were not so base as he was: that loyalty's having no meaning to him did not mean that it had none to others. Those evil men succeed best, who know well the power of love and goodness, and how to play upon them; and this Niels Goat would never learn.

As soon as the old man and his daughter had left the chamber, Dag sat up. He was wondering whether he ought to wake the poacher, when he noticed that Black Lars had opened his eyes.

Lars stretched and yawned with so much vigor, that Dag began to suspect that he might have heard what Niels Goat had said. Yet the poacher acted as if nothing were amiss. Silently, he motioned for the boy to sit down beside him and eat. While they ate, Lars looked thoughtfully at the boy, but still he said nothing.

"Why do you call him Niels *Goat?*" the boy asked when they had finished eating.

"We make up nicknames because a man's Christian name tells so little about him. Niels got his because he prances like a goat and smells worse than two." The poacher looked around the grave chamber. "I was given mine because of the color of my hair, and because some say that my father was a gypsy."

Dag studied the poacher's face. His hair certainly was black. It was long and fell to his shoulders in curls. While the boy was weighing the possibility of his being half gypsy, the poacher abruptly began to speak as if they had been arguing.

"When I was your age, my supper was often a beating and my breakfast I drew from the well." The words were said as an accusation.

Dag was about to protest that he, too, had often gone to bed hungry; but at that moment Lars's wife returned. She had been running and was out of breath. The sight of the man and the boy sitting quietly by the fire angered her.

"Get up, both of you, or Lars will be in irons before night, and I shall be a widow by Midsummer."

The poacher smiled and said, "And before Christmas you shall be wed again."

This did not still his wife's anger nor had it been meant to. "Ay, and this time I shall marry a man with a house of his own!" She shouted so loudly that she woke the baby. Her daughter's crying seemed to calm Lars's wife; she picked the child up and began to rock it in her arms. "My father has gone to tell about your hiding place."

"I guessed as much. Last night he smelled not only of goat but of fox as well. I have decided to send the boy to Bodil. She has some skins of mine which she'd better get rid of."

"Why send the boy? Go yourself and stay with her!"

Black Lars shook his head, as if this gesture were the only comment of which her remark was worthy. She glanced angrily at Dag and then kissed her own child. "Poor little one, you might as well have been father-less." The woman said no more, for Black Lars had suddenly risen; and Dag thought that he was about to hit her.

"Collect what we can carry; the rest we'll let the red cock crow over." He looked with regret at his stack of traps and bird nets, the work of many a winter night. "You follow me," he said turning to Dag, "and I will show you the road to Frederiks Castle, and tell you what to do once you get there."

Dag wanted to stay; but he obediently put on his boots and found his cap. The dog was standing next to the tunnel waiting for them.

Outside, the sun was shining and the poacher sniffed the air as a hunting dog does for the scent of a hare. Black Lars took long strides and Dag had difficulty keeping up with him. The boy's head was filled with questions, but he had neither the breath nor the courage to ask them.

"A woman's heart is made of jealousy," Black Lars unexpectedly declared and then grinned. "Bodil Karensdaughter is my wife's cousin; yet Inger cannot hear her name without her claws getting ready to scratch. Keep away from women, for they cause a man nothing but trouble," Black Lars said in that solemn tone in which most foolish advice is given.

"What is Bodil Karensdaughter like?" Dag asked with misgiving, for her cousinhood with the poacher's wife was not a promise of anything pleasant.

"She's a widow. She keeps a table where hungry men may eat, if they are hearty; and all men may drink, if they have a copper to pay. You mind what she tells you and you'll fare well." This was said kindly and seriously, Black Lars having already forgotten the advice he had just given the boy.

"Am I to stay with her?" Dag asked, for he hoped that he was only to bring the message, and then return to join the poacher.

"She'll keep you, because I sent you. There's food enough to feed a boy from the leftovers, in such a place."

They walked on without speaking. The boy was dreading the moment when he would be left alone; and Lars was silently planning his own flight.

Slowly the forest became less dense and they skirted several small fields. Every so often Black Lars would stop and cock his head. The forest was filled with all the sounds of spring, as if everything that had come to life, when the snow began to melt, wanted to tell of its existence. When the poacher halted to listen, Satan would do the same; and the man looked questioningly at the dog, before they continued on their way.

"We're here," Black Lars said softly. The boy lifted his head and looked about him with surprise; they were still in the forest, but ahead there was an open area larger than any they had passed.

The poacher placed his hand on the boy's shoulder and made Dag stand directly in front of him. "There," he said and pointed to a large oak tree growing alone in the distance. "The road is just beyond that tree. Follow it west and you'll be in Frederiks Castle by midday. You can ask anyone where Bodil Karens-daughter lives. Tell her that I am gone from the forest and I shall send a message to her later. Tell her that she must get rid of the skins, for her place will be searched when mine is found empty."

Dag glanced towards the oak tree and then pleadingly up at the poacher. Black Lars reached into his tunic and took out Dag's tin cup. As he handed it to him he said, "Remember, if you behave well, no one will give you a nickname: Dag will do." The boy smiled, even though he was frightened.

"If your back is straight, no stick will be able to bend it." The poacher believed what he was saying and therefore his voice was earnest. Let other philosophers tell of the reeds that bend; their arguments may be cleverer, but their conclusions will be no truer than Lars's.

The poacher clasped Dag's hand, as if he were parting with a grownup; then without looking back, he vanished almost at once among the trees. The dog re-

mained for a few moments with the boy, as if it wanted
to say, 'Come, let us follow him.' But when he heard
his master's whistle, Satan, too, was gone.

The boy ran as quickly as he could to the oak tree,
so that if he couldn't find the road, there would still be
hope of his being able to catch up with Black Lars. But
there it was, just as the poacher had said it would be,
running almost perfectly east-west, and in very sorry
condition. The ruts from the wheels of wagons and
carts were deep and water-filled.

Dag walked rapidly along the side of the road until
he came to a dip which the melting snow had turned
into a pool. In the middle of it stood an abandoned
wagon loaded with firewood. He stood still and stared at
it; then he picked up a stone and aimed it at the wagon;
but it fell short of its mark. He found a smaller stone,
but it was too light and flew above the wagon. His
fourth stone hit the rim of one of the wheels; and the
boy told himself that this was a sign that he would have
good luck.

He took a few hesitant steps closer to the water; and
then he began to doubt that it was such a good omen,
after all. As he approached the edge of the pool, his feet
sank deeply into the mud and water poured into his
boots. Twice he almost fell as he skirted the pool.
When he finally was around it, he sat down on an em-
bankment, to empty the water from his boots and scrape
the mud off of them.

Suddenly he heard the sound of horses' hoofs coming

from the west, from the direction of Frederiks Castle. At first he could not make up his mind whether he ought to hide; but caution at last made him pick up his boots, and crawl barefooted under some bushes. The wet snow soaked through his woolen drawers, and he was about to climb out again, when the riders came into view. There were five of them: three were peasants riding ordinary farm horses; leading them was a man who was wearing a leather jerkin and a hat with a feather in it; and beside him, on a grey mare whose back looked broken, rode Niels Goat.

CHAPTER NINE

Frederiks Castle

As DAG NEARED Frederiks Castle the forest disappeared; and the road bore evidence of greater traffic, by being so rutted, that it looked as though it had been plowed. The boy walked along the edge, dutifully kicking all the smaller stones. He was so preoccupied with his task that he did not notice the other traveler, until he was almost upon him. Sitting on the stump of a tree was a young man, dressed in black, who was stringing a lute. Dag had never seen such an instrument before; and he stood still, staring at it.

While Dag was deciding whether he should talk to the stranger or just walk on, the young man started to play. Dag waited politely, believing that it would be rude to pass him without a greeting, and ruder to interrupt his song:

> *Come, ye maidens,*
> *Come ye near,*
> *Be not shy*
> *My song to hear.*

Among thorns
The rose is found
As love will grow
On barren ground.

No man is free
Until a slave he be,
For from sweet love
He cannot flee.

So, maidens fair,
Who in their mirrors peek
When midnight comes
Their lover to seek,

Remember that
Love's chains are weak,
They bind the strong
And free the meek.

Come, ye maidens
With hair so long,
For honey-laden
Is my song.

After he had finished singing, the man continued to strum on his lute. Dag looked at him curiously: he had coarse yellow hair and a large curved nose, which stuck out from a pockmarked face. In short, he was not handsome; but as yet, the boy didn't distinguish between beautiful and ugly. In his veins still flowed so much mother's milk, that he divided up mankind only into good and evil. He stepped forward shyly, and finally, the young man looked up.

"*Pax vobiscum,*" he announced, and held up his hand, as if he were blessing the boy.

Dag did not dare to ask the stranger what the words meant. He thought that he was probably Swedish, for his father had told him that Swedes spoke a language which was difficult for a Christian to understand.

"In God's Name," the boy said, taking off his cap, as he had seen his father do, when a stranger came to King's Acre.

"What did your ears think of my song? I have written both words and music myself."

Dag smiled and said that he thought the song very pretty. But the word "pretty" did not seem to satisfy the young man for he frowned while he spoke. "It is customary to reward a poet with some small gift: copper coins, or a piece of cheese."

Dag put his hand in his pocket. Black Lars had given him some dried deer's meat. He was about to offer it to the young man, when the singer began to talk again excitedly. "The song which your untrained and unmusical ear had the privilege of listening to, was inspired by my great love . . ." The singer paused and then whispered, "For a noble and very beautiful lady."

Dag nodded to show that he understood, and the young man pointed his finger at the boy. "Curtailed as you are by years and lack of experience, you do not comprehend me." Then he declared loudly, while he struck a chord on his lute, "*Odio et amo.*"

Dag's astonishment made the young man laugh, and

the boy noticed that there was also laughter in the young man's pale blue eyes. This gave him courage, to ask the singer whether he was a Swede.

Now the young man laughed even more gaily. "The words are Latin; and mean that the young lady cannot bear to see my face, which also means that I cannot bear her either — except that I love her. Latin is a very economical language. It saves your breath. I studied it for a whole year; but like the young lady, it didn't love me. I was always *amo*ing when I should have been *amas*ing. Besides, I had no more money and no patron to pay for my studies."

Dag did not know what "patron" meant, and he was not even sure that he could tell what studies were; but he had learned that the reward for showing his ignorance was laughter, so he said nothing.

"I have composed sixteen songs in her honor. Would you like to hear another one?"

Dag nodded, though he was disappointed that the young man's songs were not like those his mother had sung to him.

The singer started to pluck the strings of the lute. As he sang, he closed his eyes, which Dag thought made him look so funny, that the boy had to turn his head away in order not to laugh out loud.

The rose is guarded by the thorn,
As pride the heart will keep
From being out of season shorn
By hands too frail and weak.

Oh, maiden with eyes so clear,
Who locks her heart with scorn,
Beware, the hand may yet be near
That picks the rose despite the thorn.

Dag, who thought that the song had ended very abruptly, looked questioningly at the singer.

"It should have been longer," the man agreed at once. "I intended to compose sixteen verses: one for every year of her life. But the night I wrote it, it was very cold and it snowed. I was on my way from Elsinore to Gurre; and had some kind farmer not taken me in, I might have frozen to death. That very night another man did freeze to death. They found him the next day near the ruins of the old castle. Love songs need warmth and a filled stomach, as well as inspiration."

Again the boy recalled the deer's meat and this time he took it out of his pocket and cut it in two with his knife.

The singer stuffed the meat that Dag had given him in his mouth at once. It was obvious that his hunger was of recent origin. For hunger is a dragon with seven heads, the first is the most ferocious but the least dangerous.

"And where are you traveling to, young man?" the singer asked.

"To Frederiks Castle." Then without warning Dag added, "My mother and father are dead. We had nothing to eat, and both the horses died, and even the black cow."

The stranger's forehead became wrinkled; but his lips were upturned as if he were about to smile. At last he bowed his head and mumbled, "May Christ have mercy on their souls."

Dag closed his tear-filled eyes and took off his cap; then he bent his head so far forward that he almost fell.

"My name is Peter Gram," the young man said softly. "I was born near Nyborg . . . 'New Castle' . . . which is one of the oldest castles in Denmark, contrary to its name. My father was a trumpeter there, but he came from Gram in Jutland. My father is dead, too; and so is my mother."

"May Christ have mercy on their souls," Dag repeated. It gave him a feeling of companionship with Peter Gram, to know that he, too, had no parents.

Peter, hiding his smile, took off his cap and again bowed his head. "Come, let's go on together. We'll follow each other as if you were my shadow and I were yours. For I am sure that God has meant us to be brothers." The singer stood up and stretched; he was very tall and thin.

"My name is Dag of King's Acre. My father rented his farm from King Christian," the boy said proudly.

"Dag is a good name," Peter said merrily. "One that even can be used at night."

Peter and Dag were climbing a hill; when they came to the top of it, they had their first glimpse of the castle. It was afternoon and the many windows glistened, reflecting the glory of the spring sun. Frederiks Castle is like a fairy castle: a castle you see in your dreams, which disappears when you open your eyes. The lake which surrounds it was still frozen, and yet the castle made Dag and Peter think of summer, when swans would swim there. Although it had bastions, it was not a fortress speaking of war; and you could not believe that there were dungeons beneath its towers. No, this castle was meant for love and children's laughter.

"It is beautiful!" Peter exclaimed. "Come, I am sure tonight that we shall feast on roasted ox and wines from Spain. The King has done well."

And Peter Gram quickened his pace so much, that Dag made his entrance into the village, which lay on the west side of the castle, running.

CHAPTER TEN

Bodil's "Tavern"

THE KING is very fond of music. He plays the flute himself. I shall beg him to give me a position worthy of my talent; then I shall teach you how to play the flute, and before long we shall go clad in furs, when it is cold, and silk in the summer. My little friend, believe me, we shall live as a couple of princes in the kingdom of music."

Dag listened attentively to his new companion, and found no fault with his logic, though the boy did not know what silk was.

"First, we must find a place to sleep for the night, where there's a fire that's kept burning. For the truth is that we are not horses, and stables are not the best places for us to sleep."

They were entering a little square. Peter looked critically at the row of low buildings; their being so near the castle made them appear more humble than they were.

"Shouldn't we go to the King right away?" Dag suggested hopefully.

Peter glanced up at the castle and then down at the boy. "When approaching kings, it is very important to pick the right moment. They are very touchy; and should we, for instance, come when the King had a stomachache, he might have our heads chopped off."

"But how does one know when the right moment comes? How shall we find out when the King does not have a stomachache?" Dag was deeply disappointed to hear that kings could suffer from pains, especially in their stomachs.

"The cook," Peter said loudly and looked at the castle admiringly. "One has to get to know the cook. He is the key that opens all doors. When the King is feeling particularly well, he sends an order to the cook for a goose to be roasted, and served with a flagon of wine; then his thoughts will bend towards music and we shall ask to see him."

Dag smiled, although the singer's picture of the domestic life of the King was very different, indeed, from that which the boy had imagined. He had thought of the King as a tall, grave man, who cared little for food and drink; and spent his days sitting on a golden throne, meting out justice: rewarding virtue and punishing evil.

"You wouldn't, by some lucky chance, have any relatives here? An aunt or an uncle?" The singer looked anxiously around at the houses, which all seemed to be glaring back at him in a most unfriendly way. "Someone who has ample provisions and a kind heart?"

Dag glanced down at his feet. He did not want to look at Peter Gram, while he was making up his mind whether he ought to trust him. He would have parted readily with his own secrets, but he was determined not to reveal any of those of Black Lars.

"There is a woman named Bodil Karensdaughter, but I don't know whether she has a good heart," the boy said finally.

"Is she old or young?" Peter asked enthusiastically. He did not seem to notice that they were being surrounded by a crowd of children. "No doubt this Bodil is as old as the devil's grandmother," Peter continued gaily, "and twice as ugly. Those who can choose are not beggars. Let's go and find her. Where does she live?"

Dag turned around and asked the oldest boy if he knew where the house of Bodil Karensdaughter was. The boy did not answer; and all the children laughed, as if asking directions, in a place so small as Frederiks Castle, proved the strangers to be fools.

A girl who had been standing a little apart from the others came hesitantly forward. "My name is Kirsten," she said. "I'll take you there." She was very dirty and Dag thought she might be a gypsy child. To his astonishment, she took his hand as if she were his sister; while behind them the other children screamed with laughter.

All the buildings in the village were small but they were not equally poor. Some had several windows, painted doors, and proud roofs that told of good oak beams beneath the thatch; while others had no more than a single window, and walls and roofs in need of repair.

The girl led them to a cottage that had no window at all; had it not been for the chimney, with the smoke rising above it, one would have assumed that it was a pigsty or a cowshed. The girl pointed to the door and Dag noticed that, like the barn door at King's Acre, it had leather, not iron, hinges; and that the wood had been neither planed nor painted. Peter and Dag exchanged glances and the man knocked at the door.

The third time he struck it more forcefully, and the door was opened a few inches. A woman's voice asked them what they wanted. Peter, who knew no more about the woman than her name, mumbled something about food and shelter. Dag fearing that the door was about to be closed again, exclaimed louder than he had intended, "I come from Black Lars."

At once, the door was flung open and the woman invited them to come in. Kirsten, whom Dag and Peter had almost forgotten, darted in ahead of them; and they discovered that the girl belonged there, for the woman slapped her. Kirsten did not even whimper. She skipped to the fireplace, and sat down on a three-legged milking stool.

The room was very dark, for the only daylight came through a small square opening in the gable, which, instead of glass, had a pig's bladder stretched across it. The woman was not alone. Two men — one of them clean-shaven, the other with a big bushy beard, and both wearing leather jerkins — were seated at a large plank table that filled almost half the room. The benches that stood alongside it could seat ten customers; for Bodil's hut was a tavern, where soldiers, and the artisans who worked at the castle, came to drink. She had no permit to keep such a place; but it was whispered that she knew the Commandant of the castle. This Bodil neither affirmed nor denied. To the right of the fireplace there was a small chest; and in the corner there were two sacks stuffed with straw for sleeping. There were no other furnishings, unless the barrel of beer, that took up the final bit of wall space, could be called furniture.

"You come from my friend," Bodil whispered urgently to Peter. Being in her middle twenties, she was neither young nor old, but she was strangely beautiful. Her hair was black and plaited around her head; her eyes were dark blue, and her lips red.

Peter made no attempt to conceal his amazement or his delight. He stood staring at her with wide eyes and open mouth. He had not heard her question and the boy's reply, in his clear child's voice, took him aback.

"I come from Black Lars," Dag said.

Bodil looked at him furiously, grabbed one of his arms, and twisting it behind him, dragged him outside. "You must not mention his name, where others can hear you," she said angrily, as soon as she had closed the door.

The boy was so frightened that he wanted to run away, but Bodil held him firmly in her grasp. "Over here," she muttered; and led him to a small shed a few steps away from the house, where she kept a pig and stored her firewood. Once they were inside, she let go of his arm and even smiled to give him courage.

"Has anything happened to Lars?" she asked anxiously.

The boy shook his head and then nodded. The pig grunted and pushed its snout up against the row of branches which kept it penned.

"Keep quiet!" Bodil whirled around, and kicked the pig to emphasize her command. Turning again to Dag, she said softly, "Speak up, child."

Dag began by telling her how the poacher had found him in the forest, and taken him to the grave chamber. He recounted all he could remember about Niels Goat's visit; and ended by relating what he had seen, only a few hours before, from his hiding place behind the bushes.

Bodil listened without interrupting. When he finished, she remarked, "Then his wife is still with him."

Dag looked at her searchingly. When he had told of Niels Goat's treachery, he had had to mention the old man's daughter; yet Bodil's gaze was still fixed intently upon him, as if she were waiting for him to answer a very important question. "She was there this morning . . . She and the baby . . ."

"She is my cousin," Bodil said. Taking the boy into her confidence, she added, "She's as jealous as a cat. Niels Goat is my mother's brother. And may the devil not wait long before claiming him, or I shall send Niels to him like a goose to be roasted. If Lars is caught, then Niels shall not live to attend service at Easter!"

As they left the shed, she took the boy's arm again.

"You must remember not to say anything to anyone!"

"The skins," Dag whispered fearfully, "I was to tell you to get rid of the skins."

She tightened her grip, so that he almost cried out in pain. "Remember what I have told you," she warned again. Opening the door to her "tavern," she pushed him roughly inside.

Peter Gram was still standing awkwardly at the door. Bodil asked him his name. The young man made a flourish with his cap, while he bowed and announced slowly, "I am Peter Gram, musician to the King."

Dag was not startled; he already understood that his newly found companion had a very friendly relationship with truth.

"If you are one of the King's musicians, why aren't you with the King?" one of the men asked sneeringly. Then he added pointedly, "We are King's men."

But once Peter's tongue was loosened, only his imagination held the bridle. He told a long tale of how the King had heard him play at Nyborg and bade him come to Frederiks Castle. He implied that his star at court was very bright; and that his ancestry was crowded with names, of which they might have heard.

Soon Bodil and her two guests, with sharp words and laughter, were driving him on to even wilder exaggerations. Dag felt sorry for the singer. Peter's lies were like a herd of oxen that had spied a green meadow: nothing could keep them back.

"Has not your friend, the King, told you that he has

gone to war against the Swedes, to make as great a fool of King Charles as you are?" one of the men at the table shouted.

"No," Peter answered. And then he did something which Dag was to hear him do many times later. He owned that most of what he had said had been lies; but he left a few falsehoods standing, and these his listeners usually believed. His stories were like an army and the singer was the general directing them, and by this stratagem he won many battles.

As the soldiers grew drunker, they became more friendly. Peter sang and played his lute. Dag, who was sitting on a bench, began to doze — for even two cups of weak beer will make a child sleepy. But when Bodil ordered Peter to sing the song about the King of England, the boy opened his eyes; and resting his head on his arms, he listened:

> *The King of England*
> *Had a daughter so fair,*
> *White as snow her hand,*
> *Yellow as gold her hair.*
> >   *Lips are red and kisses sweet*
> >   *When in gay Maytime youth will meet.*
>
> *I will ask the King of England*
> *To give me his daughter to wed*
> *And all the lands of Scotland*
> *And a gold and silver bed.*
> >   *Lips are red and kisses sweet*
> >   *When in gay Maytime youth will meet.*

And if the King my wish decline,
For kings are haughty and vain,
I'll drink his health in Frankish wine
And ask the King of Spain.
  Lips are red and kisses sweet
  When in gay Maytime youth will meet.

Soon Dag was sleeping so soundly, that he did not wake, when Peter lifted him from the bench and placed him beside Kirsten, on one of the straw-filled sacks.

CHAPTER ELEVEN

Kirsten

"Wake up!" the voice seemed to come to Dag from far away. "Wake up or I'll tickle you."

Dag opened his eyes, yawned, and then closed them again. He felt a hand trip across his chest, while another dug into his side. "You're tickling me!" He laughed, squirmed, kicked, and finally sat up. The girl, who was kneeling beside him, held her hands high in the air. Dag looked around the room; he and the girl were alone.

"Where is Peter?" he asked.

"They've gone," the girl replied and shrugged her shoulders as if to say, 'And I don't care where.'

A dim light came through the little window. Now that he was fully awake, Dag felt cold. He went to the fireplace; and he was about to sit down on the little stool, but the girl was before him. As she seated herself, she said proudly, "It is mine."

Dag picked up a stick from the floor and began to poke the fire, which was burning so brightly that there was no reason to improve it. But poking a fire is one of the best things one can do, if one wants to think; and so much had happened to Dag, during the last few days, that he wanted to remember everything in proper order, so that his mind might catch up with his body.

"You can have my stool." The little girl had risen. Dag smiled and shook his head. "But I want you to have it," she said eagerly. Dag threw his stick into the fire and sat down.

"Does your father beat you?" the girl asked very seriously.

"My father is dead," he answered solemnly; then he noticed her confused expression and added, "Peter Gram is not my father." Turning away from Kirsten he said, "My mother is dead, too. My father used to hit me sometimes when I was bad." The boy's expression became even sadder; for, though he was trying, he could only recall his father having struck him once: the time he had let the cows roam into the wheat field; and that had been more than two years ago, when he had been only five.

"Bodil hits me all the time, but she is not my mother, not really. My mother is a queen and I am a princess."

Dag looked at the girl. She was dressed in rags and he had never seen anyone as dirty. "It's not true," he said thoughtfully. "You're not a princess."

"I am!" the girl retorted. "And if you don't believe me then you can't sit on my stool."

"If your mother is a queen," he began to argue, without taking his glance from her angry face, "then why are you living here?"

Kirsten clenched her fists. "Bodil stole me away. She's a witch."

Dag recalled the strength of the woman's fingers when she held his arm.

"She can cast spells and turn herself into a cat," Kirsten whispered.

"If she could change herself into a bear or a wolf . . ." Dag suggested pensively. Once, in Elsinore, he had seen a dancing bear and it had frightened him.

"Who is more powerful: a princess or a witch?"

The girl had spoken so earnestly, that suddenly Dag realized that Kirsten was still a little child. 'As I was,' he thought, 'when I played with reeds down by the lake, and called them ships.' He knew that Bodil was the girl's mother, and that she was not a witch; but merely a woman who sold liquor to men too poor to buy it elsewhere.

"Princesses are more powerful," he said aloud. Then he remembered his own wish to see the King and tell him all that had happened that winter. It hurt him to realize that he, too, had been foolish and childish. For a moment he became an adult; he wanted to cry and he couldn't.

"When you are a princess, you can do anything you want to," Kirsten remarked thoughtfully, while she picked her nose. "Anything at all. I will tell Bodil that if she doesn't obey me, I shall have her burned as a witch."

From the small heap of kindling near the fireplace, Dag picked up a handful of twigs and threw them into the fire. They burst into flames and were gone. 'A king can do anything,' he thought. 'Is that why everyone dreams of being a king? What would I do if I were a prince? I'd make Black Lars Keeper of the Forest; and Peter Gram could sing and play . . .' But then his silent reasoning was interrupted by the thought that if he had been king, he would not have known about Black Lars nor have met Peter Gram; for he would have been off in Sweden, fighting a war against another king.

"I shall wear a red dress and golden shoes even in the morning," Kirsten exclaimed happily. "And I won't have to be good or nice ever."

Dag laughed and started to tease her, "But how do you know that the queen won't switch you? Maybe she's just as mean as Bodil."

The girl shook her head vigorously. "No, she won't! The queen is my real mother and she loves me, and it won't matter what I do . . . If I tear my red dress then she will order a new one to be sewn for me at once. And if I cry she will kiss me and give me black candies."

Both the children sat quietly for a while — Kirsten on one of the benches and Dag on her stool. Then the girl began to talk again. Her voice was low. "At night I am afraid especially when there are many men here. Now most of them have gone with the King. But sometimes there are so many. They get drunk and fight. Then I run outside, except when it is very dark and there are no stars; for when clouds cover the sky then God can't see us and the devils are about, so if it is very dark I crawl under this bench, and pray to God that

He will take me away . . . Black Lars comes here
sometimes when no one else is here. He takes me on his
knee and says he's going to marry me. And he has
candies in his pocket for me to find . . . Are you
afraid of the dark?" she asked.

Dag pondered the question long before he answered.
"Sometimes I am, when the wind blows, for then there
are voices . . . And I don't like thunder either . . .
Right near King's Acre there's a hill where a troll lives.
I never went there after the sun had set; for trolls, though
they have sharp eyes at night, can't see in the day-
time. Trolls are like cats, but I am not really frightened
of them." But the boy had no sooner said the words than
he feared that they weren't true.

Keeping her gaze upon him to prevent him from
lying, Kirsten asked slowly, "Was King's Acre a big
farm?"

Dag did not know what to reply, for he did think
that King's Acre was big; but now that he had seen
Frederiks Castle, he wasn't sure. "We had two horses
and three cows. There were pigs and some hens, but
they are all dead now. My father sold the pigs but the
hens we ate ourselves. But he wouldn't sell the cows and
the horses because, he said, without them there was no
farm. He went to Elsinore to get help and he didn't
come back. And my mother died."

Kirsten touched Dag's hand. "Maybe your faher will
come back."

"How can he if he's dead!" the boy said angrily. The

telling of the bare events of that winter made Dag miserably aware of what he had lost. "My father would have come back if he could have! If you'd known him, you would know that."

"Maybe they were not your father and mother, and you are a prince," she said softly.

Dag shook his head and tried to laugh, but his effort became a soundless grimace.

The door opened, and Kirsten moved to Dag's side. Bodil and Peter Gram entered; both of them were smiling.

"We are going to the war!" Peter exclaimed. "We shall learn to play a drum, not a flute or a lute. The sword is the proper instrument for a man to play; with it, he can win honor and gold. God has made wars for the sake of the poor, to give them a chance through honest fighting to become rich."

Dag looked up at Peter's beaming face. It surprised him that two so different men as Black Lars and the singer should have the same ideas about war, which he had heard his father so often curse. But war is a dream, and only too late, do its realities appear and awaken the dreamer.

"You are coming, my boy!" Peter continued. "Aren't we brothers? Bodil will buy some barrels of schnapps in Copenhagen; and we shall take them all the way to Christianopolis, where the King is! He will be surprised to see me," Peter said seriously, forgetting that only the children were listening and he needn't lie so much.

" 'Peter,' he will say, 'play with your sword now, as once you did on your lute, and you shall ride by my side.' "

Dag put his hands over his ears; at that moment he hated Peter Gram.

"A wooden horse is all you'll ever ride," Bodil said contemptuously.

But Peter only laughed, for he was a yeoman and had no fear of that "animal" of torture, which the noblemen sometimes condemned their peasants to "ride." He strummed on his lute and sang:

> *Master Olaf buckled his sword to his side,*
> *To follow his master so fair,*
> *And the stars behind the clouds did hide*
> *And cold as the grave was the air.*

Peter stopped singing and looked about him as if he were dazed; was it possible that he had only now realized how melancholy that song was?

"You'd better stay by the chimney corner and sing about the war; it's safer than being in it," Bodil said mockingly. But a moment later she was grinning again and she turned to Dag very good-naturedly. "The bird has flown and burned his nests. Today the gamekeeper's face is as long, as yesterday his hopes were high. They say he beat Niels Goat half to death for leading him astray. I don't understand why he stopped without finishing the job, unless the devil came to Niels's aid."

"Where is Lars now?" the boy asked.

"They say that those men who are loved by children

are also those most loved by women . . . Who knows where Black Lars is! He would not be so foolish as to leave a trail behind him."

Kirsten whispered to the boy anxiously, "You will come too, won't you?"

Dag looked with astonishment at the girl; he had not even thought that he might have a choice. Then he nodded and she smiled happily.

CHAPTER TWELVE

The Mercenaries

FAR, FAR TO THE NORTH stretches King Charles's kingdom of Sweden. North, beyond the dark forests to where the reindeer lives and winter never leaves. North to the land of the Lapps, who know magic and can speak the language of animals. To reach the northernmost point of King Charles's realm, you must travel as far as if you had as a goal the Palaces of the Pope, who lives in Rome where oranges grow and snow never falls.

Three counties of Denmark are separated from the rest of the kingdom by the Sound, and have a border in common with the realm of King Charles. Once, a Danish Queen, the good Margarete, did rule all the lands of the north. Both the King of Sweden and our King Christian the Fourth carry three crowns on their shields: one for Norway, one for Denmark, and one for Sweden. And now because each would like to make a reality of his shield's claim, they have engaged their people in a war; and the wolves in the forest sniff the air, for every battle is their victory.

It had taken Bodil, Peter, and the children more than

three weeks to get from Frederiks Castle to Skaane, the most southern of the three counties. Obtaining passage had been difficult because there was still drift ice in the Sound, making that short voyage only possible for larger ships. When finally they reached Landskrona, more troubles awaited them: They needed a cart and a horse; and in wartime even the oldest nag becomes valuable. Bodil did succeed in purchasing a mare; but by what means and at what price, neither Peter nor the children knew.

Armies neither sow nor reap, but they eat heartily. Although the war had but started, the people of Skaane had learned to hide what they owned and trust no strangers. The German and Scottish regiments that King Christian had hired, because he could not raise a large enough army among the Danes, cared little for the honor of war but much for the spoils. If they were hungry, they wanted to be fed; and if they were cold, they wanted wood for their fires.

In May begin the light nights: the magic summer of the north, when for a few months darkness is conquered. Even at midnight the sky is pale and only the strongest stars are to be seen. Yet these nights can be chilly. After the sun has set you can feel the final breath of winter.

Peter Gram had built a fire and they were all sitting around it, staring into the flames. They had traveled far that day, yet none of them wanted to sleep. Peter was playing his lute and singing a ballad about a woman who had married the King of the Elves; now he had reached the final verse:

For she had wedded the fairy king
And taken his golden ring.
Her children's voices she ne'er will hear
As the dew weeps its pearly tear,
Nor will she sleep in her good man's bed
When winter comes and the world is dead.
For she has wedded the fairy king
And taken his golden ring.

The sweet melody as well as the words of the song
made Dag dream. Last summer, down by the little pool,
near the cluster of birch trees at King's Acre, he had seen
the King of the Elves. The sun had set and a mist had
spread over the water. Suddenly, though there was no
wind, the mist began to move and it looked like a giant
man, as tall as the trees. There, in the center of the white
vapor, had been the King of the Elves, coming slowly
towards him. Frightened, the boy had run home; but
now he imagined that he had stayed and spoken to the
King of the Elves. So absorbed was Dag in his day-
dream, that he didn't hear the horses' hoofs.

"*Grüss Gott!*"

Dag turned his attention from the fire and glanced
towards the road. Four horsemen — that is, four horses
and five men, for two of the men rode on one horse —
had halted near Bodil's cart.

"*Du bist danen?*"

Again their officer spoke. Dag, who had not understood his salutation, looked at the man with amazement.
He was at least a head taller than any other man the
boy had ever seen. He had a big bushy red beard. His

voice was very deep and masterful. Dag wondered whether he might be King Christian the Fourth of Denmark, and his heart began to beat very quickly.

Peter Gram took a few steps towards the bearded officer. Once more his strong voice was heard. *"Ver-dammt land!"* This was followed by a dozen English curses, for the officer was a Scot.

Frightened and thoroughly confused, Peter started to back away from the strangers. He had never heard English spoken before; and yet it sounded familiar, as if he ought to have understood it. The mercenaries usually spoke German, no matter where they came from; even among the Danish troops, commands were given in that language because many of the officers were noblemen from Schleswig and Holstein.

"Gruïss Gott, we are peaceful travelers," the singer said very slowly in German.

All of the soldiers laughed. *"Verdammt travelers!"* the officer shouted.

Suddenly the man who had been riding behind his comrade leapt from his uncomfortable seat, and ran towards Bodil's mare, who was grazing just beyond the fire.

"In the name of the King of Denmark, we take your horse!" the red-bearded man shouted in English and laughed.

"We are peaceful travelers," Peter protested in German.

"A peaceful traveler, whom we shared our food with last night, stole our comrade's horse while we were all asleep," said one of the soldiers, who spoke German well.

Peter held out his lute as though it were an offering. "But it was not we who stole your horse." The soldier turned away without answering.

Kirsten had hidden underneath the cart. Dag, who had concealed himself behind it, now joined her in order to get a better view without being seen by the soldiers. The girl put her hand on his neck and he pushed it away. "They'll take the horse," she whispered.

Dag was watching Bodil. From the cart, she had taken the whip with which she beat the horse and sometimes the children. She was holding it behind her back. Never for an instant did her gaze leave the man who was leading her mare by its forelock towards his companions. Suddenly she gave a sharp cry, ran forward, and struck his hand with the whip. He screamed in pain and released the animal. The mare turned and Bodil brought the whip down hard on its rump. Wildly the horse broke into a canter and ran across the field till a stone fence finally stopped its flight; then it started to graze as if nothing at all had happened.

The disappointed soldier drew his sword; the flames from the fire reflecting in the weapon turned its color from silver to red. He hesitated and looked towards his commanding officer. Red Beard was laughing so uproariously that Dag thought he might fall off his horse.

Without fear of the soldier or his sword, Bodil screamed angrily, "That horse is mine!"

The officer stopped laughing. With a wave of his

hand he ordered the soldier to sheathe his sword; then he drew his pistol from his belt and examined it, blowing into the muzzle to clean the barrel. Very slowly he loaded the weapon, making sure that no step in the process was missed by the spectators.

The soldiers looked on with the same kind of expectation mirrored on their faces, as is to be seen on the features of peasants when they watch tumblers perform in the marketplace. When Red Beard had reached the point where he was to select the bullet, he looked long into his pouch. First he picked up one bullet and then another, letting each drop with a shake of his head. Finally, he found one that satisfied him, and he held the bullet up between his thumb and forefinger to show it to everyone; then he kissed it before inserting it in the barrel.

Red Beard leveled the pistol at Bodil's chest. Her face turned white; but she pinched her lips together in defiance and uttered not a sound.

The whole world was quiet; even the horses felt the importance of the moment and stood still with their ears pricked up.

The explosion shattered the silence. One of the horses reared and almost threw its rider. A long tongue of fire shot out from the mouth of the pistol.

Peter Gram ran forward with his arms outstretched to catch Bodil when she fell. But she did not fall; she looked at her unharmed chest and then up at Red Beard. Smiling he stuck the pistol back into his belt; then he placed his right hand on his nose and drew out from one of his nostrils, the bullet. He gazed at it for a moment as if he, too, were surprised to find it in such an unlikely place, then he returned it to his bullet pouch.

The soldiers laughed, the officer laughing the loudest; his white teeth gleaming in the forest of his red beard. He only stopped when he spied Kirsten, who having crawled out from underneath the cart, was staring at him with terror-filled eyes.

"*Kleine madchen*," he said, and the tremor in his voice as he said the words "little girl" made them sound like an apology. In spite of her fury, Bodil forced herself to smile.

"He's about as amusing as a cat is to a mouse," Peter muttered.

Bodil had taken the stoneware jug from the cart and was filling Dag's tin cup with schnapps. When the liquor all but reached the brim, she handed it to Red Beard.

"*Verdammt* woman, you can ride with me. I will make you my sergeant," he exclaimed, and draining the cup, he gave it back to her.

"Bring four wooden cups," she called over her shoulder. Although these were smaller than the tin cup, she filled them only half way up. Peter handed them to the soldiers. The soldier, whose wrist was still smarting from the lash of Bodil's whip, grumbled, but he accepted the drink.

When Peter returned to the cart, Bodil asked him to hold the jug, and he noticed that her hand was trembling. 'So you were afraid,' he thought; but a moment later, he wasn't sure, for the jug was so heavy that carrying it a long time would make anyone's hands shake.

With the drinking of the liquor, the danger was past. Dag, who wanted to see the swords that the men were wearing, timidly approached the soldiers; and Red Beard smiled at him.

The soldiers were from a Scottish regiment, though they did not all hail from that barren land. Two were from Mecklenburg and one from Holstein. The red-bearded officer was a Scotsman. He called himself a lord and said that he was the son of an earl, though his father still lived the peaceful life of a shepherd in northern Scotland. He had acquired his title the day he landed on the continent. Among the foreign troops, he was not the only one, who had reached high rank in his native country by the mere act of leaving it. Bodil knew this well, for there were often mercenaries at Frederiks Castle. She knew, too, that the easiest way of entering their good graces was to pretend to believe their lies; for the less claim a man has to his title, the more he prides himself on it.

"I beg you for protection," Bodil said and offered the officer the filled tin cup once more. "I am a weak woman, the mother of two children."

The Scot stroked his beard. When he had emptied the cup, he smacked his lips; then, leaning down towards her, he held out his hand in a lordly manner for her to kiss. Bodil played her part and kissed it. She called Dag and Kirsten, who obediently followed her example.

The officer smiled pleasantly for he was genuinely fond of children.

"Who is that man?" he asked pointing to Peter.

"I am a singer, traveling to court," Peter replied and bowed.

Red Beard requested a song but not a long one, for they had far to travel that night. Peter sang a ballad about a nobleman who follows his king to the wars, leaving behind his wife and children. The lady is falsely told that her husband has died; in sorrow, she drinks poison just as her good man comes riding over the drawbridge.

The Scottish "lord" was pleased, and he threw Peter Gram a large copper coin. Saying that they would meet again in Christianopolis, he bade them Christ's Peace and rode away.

When the horses' hoofs could no longer be heard, Bodil turned to Peter and held out her hand. At first he seemed confused; mockingly, he bowed and kissed it. But she turned her hand palm up again and grudgingly, he gave her the copper coin.

CHAPTER THIRTEEN

The Vultures Gather

It was one of the first days of June; the sky was cloudless and the birds sang of hope. Nature is indifferent to war; even in its midst when clouds black as death should be gathering, she will arrange for summer days suited for dreams of love.

The roads of Blekinge were filled with travelers. Some rode horses and wore fine clothes; and for them the other travelers, who were their own beasts of burden, stepped out of the way. There were farmers with carts drawn by oxen; and soldiers with military supplies, loaded on wagons, which were drawn by horses that farmers had "lent" to the King — while they had given freely of their curses.

The traffic was towards the east, towards Kalmar, to which King Christian had laid siege. They were going to war, yet what they had in common, rich and poor, young and old, was a strange feeling of joy as if tomorrow were their wedding day. To understand war, one must know more of it than the dying soldier on the battlefield is willing to tell. He can but scream, "I did not want to die!" forgetting that when last he saw the red, red rose of death spread over a chest, he had shouted, "Victory!"

A little south of Mein Lake, a cart particularly old was slowly making its way in the same direction as all the others. Hidden beneath a layer of straw were a few sacks of wheat and two barrels of schnapps, which the owner hoped would bring a high price in Christianopolis, the fortress and stronghold of the Danish forces that were besieging Kalmar. Bodil — for it was her cart— walked beside it and held the reins. Peter Gram kept pace with her on the other side of the vehicle. He had been whistling; but now he was tired and he hoped that Bodil would soon call a rest. He turned around; the children were not out of sight, but they were far behind. He knew that neither the children's nor his own weariness would make Bodil stop. She herself never seemed to need rest.

"Damned witch," he muttered. He glanced at the horse. He knew that Bodil feared that it would not have the strength to reach Christianopolis.

Ahead was an unfenced field of light green grass. Bodil drove the cart off the road and examined the mare's front legs. She scowled, shook her head, and then began to unhitch the animal.

"You drive it too hard," Peter remarked while he helped her. Bodil grinned at him. The horse, once freed, took only a few steps and began to graze.

When Dag saw the cart stop he sat down on a low stone wall, which is the common form of fence in

Blekinge, where it is said that the fields grow more stones than stalks of grain. Dag's right foot felt as though there was a thorn in it. He looked at the bottom of his foot; it was so dirty that even after he had brushed the dust away, he gave up hope of being able to see anything as tiny as a thorn.

"Something hurt?" Kirsten asked. Dag did not answer. "I'm tired," she said softly.

"If you think about it, then it only gets worse," he explained though he, himself, had been thinking of little else for a very long time.

Dag caught sight of a lark that was standing still in the air; its little wings were moving so fast that he could not see them. "Do you think it is true that God sees everything we do? Do you think that He is watching us now — and them, too?" With a thrust of his head, he indicated that by "them," he meant Peter and Bodil.

The little girl was growing used to being asked strange questions, while her own very ordinary ones were left unanswered. Once when Bodil had complained and called Dag a very sullen child, Peter had said that it was because Dag's parents were dead that he appeared so serious. Kirsten looked at the boy; his face was solemn. How could she answer his question? She had received no training in religion; and the only prayer that she could say by heart, had been taught to her by a soldier who had been living with her mother. It was a strange prayer for a child to recite before she went to bed; and she connected no meaning with the words, although she found them comforting. Now she repeated the prayer to herself, hoping that it might help her to find an answer to Dag's query:

> *And if tonight I should die*
> *I pray God my soul to take*
> *And let my sins buried lie*
> *For Christ's sweet pity's sake.*

"No," she finally said. "He doesn't look all the time, only sometimes . . . He couldn't. He has to eat and to sleep and to take care of the angels."

The lark dived from the sky down to a hillock of high grass. Dag wondered whether its nest was there. He remembered that the summer before he had hunted for larks' nests, but he hadn't been able to find any.

"I don't think He sees everything either," the boy said. Again he looked towards the cart. Yesterday Bodil had beaten him with a stick and there were marks all over his body. Peter had just walked away without doing anything to protect him. Kirsten had wept silently while he was being hit; and when her mother had noticed her tears she had laughed. "When the time comes for you to marry, I'll find something better than a beggar for you!"

The word "beggar" had stung Dag as hard as the blows, for though he did not know it, he was proud. "Your mother said that I was a beggar but she is a thief. She has taken my tin cup and my boots from me." The boots Bodil had sold for a few copper coins as soon as it had been warm enough for him to go barefoot. "She is a thief!" he repeated because he was convinced that to steal was worse than to beg.

"Yes," the girl agreed, "she is a thief." But the word did not have the same force to her as it did for Dag, for she was not a peasant's child, but a thief's daughter. "We'd better catch up with them," she said, "or we won't get anything to eat."

Dag knew that the girl was right but he wanted to stay away, even at the risk of another beating. He took one of the loose stones from the fence, and threw it as far as he could. He had forgotten about the lark and now to his surprise it flew up, batting its wings; his stone must have fallen near its nest.

Kirsten climbed down and stood by the side of the road. "Bodil will get angry if we don't come."

"I don't care," he replied. But suddenly he thought that it was not only foolish but childish to remain there, and he jumped down from the wall.

On their way to the cart, Kirsten picked a yellow flower and gave it to Dag. The girl was fond of flowers; she made chains of them which she hung around her neck. One day Dag had worn one; but Peter Gram had laughed at him and so he had thrown it way. Now he carefully hid the flower in his hand, and when the girl was not looking, he dropped it in the grass.

Bodil and Peter were sitting on the ground, their backs against a wheel of the cart. Between them lay a loaf of bread and a large piece of cheese. Peter was drinking beer from a jug. Silently the children waited while Bodil cut two thick slices of bread and two small pieces of cheese. First Kirsten and then Dag were allowed to drink from the jug; but neither of them liked it, for the liquid tasted more like foul water than beer.

"Three more days and we shall be in Christianopolis," Peter said happily, stretching himself out on the ground.

Bodil glanced at the horse and then at the road, which was in very poor condition. "If the mare only holds out," she said thoughtfully, "I can sell it for sausage when we get there."

Dag, who loved the mare, felt his hatred for Bodil so keenly that he could not look at her. The horse, being spared the understanding of human words, grazed indifferently.

They had all fallen asleep, even Bodil. The rumbling of a large wagon awakened them. It was heavily loaded and drawn by four horses. Two men walked beside it, three women and several children followed it. Although the youngest woman and the children were barefoot, they were all well dressed. The older man, who held the reins, had a pistol in his belt; and his companion had a musket hanging across his back.

Peter Gram took off his cap and called, "Christ be with you!"

At first the older man merely nodded; but then he thought better of it, reined his horses, and replied, "Christ be with you." When the wagon stopped, the women stood still; and the children gathered around them like chicks around a mother hen.

"Where are you going?" Peter asked, playing the

"master" of the "family." Bodil grinned. The stranger did not reply. He was looking with contempt at Bodil's cart and horse.

Suddenly the young man started to laugh and asked Peter Gram what kind of animal was pulling his cart. Peter smiled. "A unicorn!" he said loudly. "But it's lost its horn. We ground it into powder. Would you like to buy some?"

Peter's response had confused the man and yet, in some vague way, he knew that he was being made to appear foolish; he frowned and straightened the musket on his back.

"We are peaceful merchants," the older man said. "And what are you?"

"Honest merchants," Bodil answered, "as Christ is my witness."

The old man smiled, but his features weren't used to it, and soon he scowled again. "Are you on your way to Kalmar?"

"I cannot enter a besieged city," she said.

"Our King Christian — May Christ bless his cause! — took the town of Kalmar ten days ago. The Swedish army has fled, though there are still some of King Charles's men holding Kalmar Castle. They say King Charles is dead and soon our King shall be King of Sweden."

Kalmar! The thought of the plunder there would be in such a city filled Bodil with wonder! The soldiers would be rich. If only she had twenty, not just two, barrels of schnapps!

Dag, who had heard every word, began, in spite of himself, to dream again of meeting the King.

The stranger hit one of his horses with the end of the reins and the big wagon moved on. Peter, Kirsten, Bodil, and Dag watched them as they departed. Kirsten waved, and one of the children walking behind the cart, a boy of about ten, stuck out his tongue.

CHAPTER FOURTEEN

The Beggars' Army

THE SECOND TIME that the mare fell, Bodil did not bother to use the whip. The animal was breathing heavily. Peter unhitched it but still it did not get up. With great difficulty they pushed the cart off the road. Peter took a handful of straw and wiped the sweat from its flanks. "We should have stayed a whole day at the last place and given her some rest," he said.

Bodil spat at the horse. She was furious. She was like a captain who, at the moment he is ready to hoist anchor and set sail, discovers that his crew has run away. Now that there was only a day's journey to Christianopolis, a dying horse seemed to her like a mutiny.

"May the devil take it!" she cursed. "There's nobody to sell it to here, and if it dies a natural death we'll just have to leave it in the fields to rot." Then she spoke to the mare threateningly, "You'll be unclean only the executioner may skin you." She waited as if she expected the animal to reply, then angrily she turned and walked away.

"Come on," Peter whispered into the mare's ear.

"Come on, my beauty." He patted its neck, while he pulled its forelock gently. The horse tried to rise. Twice it fell back, but the third time it managed to stand. With his arm around its neck, Peter led it off the road. There was fresh grass in the field but the mare didn't seem to care. It was as if she knew that she was dying and had ceased to dream of oats or green grass.

"Will she die?" Dag asked. He had already asked the same question twice that day, but Peter had pretended that he had not heard him.

Now looking at the boy and realizing how much he cared, he said, "It has no eternal soul as we have . . . It does not suffer."

To Dag "eternal" was a meaningless sound, but "soul" he understood. "They do feel pain," he argued.

"I am telling you what the Bishop of Odense says," Peter replied.

"It's a lie!" Dag retorted; but he knew that a bishop was a splendid man about whom a child might not use the word "lie," so he added, "He just doesn't know."

Peter smiled, "But, Dag, it says the same thing in the Catechism of Luther."

What Dag knew of the teaching of Our Lord and Martin Luther came from his mother, who could neither read nor write. In his whole life, the boy had been inside a church only three times, and one of them had been when he was three weeks old. "We are all alike: horses, birds, and men," he said.

Kirsten who had been listening remarked, "But not spiders!"

"No," the boy agreed, "spiders and worms are different. Everything that has eyes, even frogs and lizards are like us."

Peter stopped smiling, for though his verses often halted, he was a poet and understood what the child meant. "The eyes are the mirror of the soul and if the mirror is there, the soul must be there, too," he said.

Suddenly the mare started to graze, as if having been given a soul by Peter and Dag, she had decided to live a little longer.

"Maybe tomorrow it can pull the cart again." Bodil's voice carried no conviction, and Peter did not disagree. She was still angry and Peter's muteness annoyed her. "Find some water," she ordered; and as the singer went to get the wooden bucket that hung from the tailboard of the cart, she said to the children, "Why haven't you gathered wood for a fire?"

Peter and the children went off together. When they were out of sight, Bodil gazed intently in every direction to make certain that no one was coming. From a nearby tree she broke off four branches and stripped them of twigs and leaves. With these four sticks she made two crosses; one she placed on the ground in front of the horse and the other behind it. She drew out the knife that she always carried in her belt and made a gash in her left arm. With the fingers of her right hand she made a cross of blood on the mare's forehead.

"Snakes and worms . . . Gall and blood . . . Christ's wounds the sickness take . . . Moon is silver. Day is gold. Devils flee . . . Christ comes, His sign is

true!" These words Bodil had learned from a woman
whom some said had sold her soul to the devil. They
were supposed to cure people who coughed blood; and
Bodil thought they might help the mare.

For a long time she stood motionless, a few feet away
from the animal, watching its every movement. Finally,
the horse noticed the cross in front of its head; it sniffed
at it, and then with its snout shoved the cross, so that it
again became only two sticks. Bodil, who had been
waiting for an omen, did not know what to make of it.
She continued staring at the mare; it seemed more lively
and Bodil decided that it had been a good omen.

Peter had found a stream, while the children were col-
lecting dead branches for kindling. The water was clear
and he could see the stones at the bottom of the brook.
He heard something behind him but he did not turn
around; he knew it was Dag and he hoped that the boy
would leave him alone.

"Peter . . ."

"Where is Kirsten?"

"Picking flowers . . ." Dag lay down in the grass.
"Why do we stay with *her*?"

Peter sighed deeply and did not answer.

"She took your money away from you! Why did
you let her?"

"She took your tin cup and your boots and you didn't
do anything," Peter replied. "You didn't run away."
He could not look at the boy. He knew how foolish
his answer had been. Dag had not run away because he

was a child. Only children who have always eaten well, always had a bed to sleep in, and never feared the coming of winter, have dreams of being alone; for they have no knowledge of the ways of the world to curb their fancy.

Dag had hid his face in his arms. Suddenly he lifted his head and blurted, "But I am only a boy and you are a man!"

The singer laughed, "Am I a man?"

He turned the wooden bucket over and sat down on it. Dag looked at Peter, 'If she were here, he wouldn't dare do that,' the boy thought.

"Sometimes I think that I am a man, but then it is mostly in my dreams . . . The dreams I have now are the same I had when I was a child. But now they are bitter for I know that they are daydreams . . . But still I dream. Sometimes I think that dreams and poetry — and even my lute — are a cross like the one Our Blessed Saviour carried . . . My brother, who is older than I am, is a blacksmith and knows the nature of iron. He listens to a song as a man drinks a pint of beer; he will not get drunk on it as I do. He is much respected and people will ride many a mile to have their horses shod by him. He is a man. I wish I were like him." Peter looked down at the brook; it reflected the blue sky. He laughed and in his laughter there was no bitterness.

"No! I do not want to be like him. Blessed are the trees, for from their wood, man can construct a lute or make a cross. Blessed is the sun and blessed is the sky

and blessed are fools like me." Peter held out his hand to
Dag.

The boy turned away. He knew now that Peter
would not leave Bodil Karensdaughter; and Dag was too
young to forgive such weakness.

When Peter, Kirsten, and Dag came back to the field
a strange and wonderful sight met their eyes. The cart
was surrounded by ten people — seven men and three
women — while Bodil stood on top of it, brandishing a
cudgel at her besiegers. They were screaming and
spitting at her, but she was holding them at bay. They
were the kind of men and women that you pass in
the streets of Elsinore without seeing; only on Sunday do you notice them, when they are standing on
the steps of the church waiting for alms. One was miss-
ing an arm, another an eye, and there were not a dozen
teeth among the lot of them. Their clothes were rags.
Only their hunger and their thirst were whole and real.

At first Peter could not help smiling, for each of the
"soldiers" in the army of beggars seemed so pathetic
that Bodil did not appear to be in any danger; but they
were ten, and ten dogs can kill a wolf. He motioned
to the children to be silent and follow him. Peter found
a branch almost as long as he was tall. He pointed to a
stick and Dag picked it up. As quietly as they could
the three of them advanced.

One of the women was throwing a stone at Bodil;
but the stone was too large or the woman too weak, for
it missed its mark and struck the side of the cart. The

woman bent down to find another stone. Peter hit her from behind, and she shrieked as she fell forward, though she was more frightened than hurt.

Suddenly Bodil jumped off the cart and started swinging her cudgel among the beggars. They retreated in disorder but they did not flee. They ran no further than the other end of the field; there they stood huddled together.

While Peter prepared the fire, he watched them out of the corner of his eye. When he went to the cart to get the little box that contained the flint and steel, he said to Bodil, "Maybe we should give them something to drink . . . to make them leave."

"I'll give them nothing but bruises, so they won't come back for more!" she replied.

Silently, he took the tinderbox. He knew that Bodil was right. To give the beggars a little to drink, was to whet their appetites, and give them that bit of courage they needed.

The sun set. The pallid northern summer night, soft and yet more colorless than twilight, began. Ever so slowly the beggars were making their way towards the fire around which Bodil, Peter, and the children were sitting. They were desperate, not so much from hunger as from thirst; a thirst that could not be quenched in the clear water of a brook.

They are the people who ride a nightmare even when the sun is in the sky; and the only thing that gives them peace is strong drink. Such people are always to be found where there is an army. They live off begging, stealing, or doing a chance service. The Commandant of Christianopolis had expelled them from the fortress two days before, and since then they had had nothing to drink. As the soldiers drove them at sword's point across the drawbridge, they had appeared pitiable; but now their desperation made them bold.

Bodil and the children were surprised by the first stone, although Peter had been expecting an attack. Kirsten cried out in pain; a rock had grazed her shoulder. The beggars shouted as if they had won a great victory. Dag took Kirtsen's hand and they ran to the cart. Although the girl was not badly hurt, she could not stop crying.

The beggars did not take careful aim; screaming and shouting, they picked up the nearest stick or stone and threw it. Peter and Bodil took up battle, and while casting stones against their attackers, they made their way to the protection of the cart.

In the distance there was a horseman. The beggars had their back to the rider, and did not know of his approach, until he was almost upon them. At full gallop the man rode towards the army of beggars with his sword drawn. They shrieked and ran in all directions. A lame man and two women, who were unable to run, threw themselves on their knees in front of the horseman, as he dismounted. He raised his sword as if he were about to strike, while they begged for mercy.

"Kill them!" Bodil screamed.

The man lowered his sword slowly and put it back in his belt. Too fear-filled to move, the beggars waited

silently; then with bowed heads they started to crawl away. As soon as they reached the road, they stood up and hobbled away as quickly as they could.

"Bodil Karensdaughter!" The rider shouted and led his horse towards the cart. It was Black Lars!

CHAPTER FIFTEEN

The Silver Mark

EVERYONE in Frederiks Castle had known of Black Lars's escape and the beating which the new gamekeeper and his helpers had given Niels Goat, when they found the grave chamber empty. But where the poacher and his family had gone, and how he came to be riding along the road to Kalmar and Christianopolis, on a fine horse, and outfitted with sword and musket, were mysteries, only Black Lars could explain. And he demanded food and drink as payment for their rescue, before he would answer any of their questions. Bodil, who had not failed to notice Lars's horse and was already making plans in which the animal played an important role, did not stint on either bread or beer. The children, who had never seen her so merry, were quick to take advantage of her mood to get a second supper.

Black Lars took a deep draught of beer and after he had swallowed it, he smacked his lips. "I knew what he had come for . . . I saw it in his eyes every time he looked at me." He lifted the cup again and drank. "If I had thought Niels Goat worth hanging for, I would have killed him. As it is, I owe him thanks for being so kind as to warn me; for if he had not come, I might have worn the hempen collar." Black Lars scratched his neck as if he could feel the rope.

"But Niels Goat had not come to warn you!" Dag said excitedly. Whatever faults Black Lars had — and being human, he had many — they were not easily observed by a child's eye.

"No, Dag, that wasn't why he had come; but neither does the fleeing deer intend to leave tracks for the hunter to follow. I saw in Niels Goat's eyes what Our Lord must have seen when he looked at Judas . . . Niels thought that if he could get my wife to leave me of her own free will, then they could share all the riches he believed I had, and get the five silver marks, as well. For Niels loves to dream of the wealth of others, and he thought my purse was a great deal heavier than it is." Black Lars laughed and held up his purse. It was a small leather bag tied with a thong. Lars opened it and took out a silver mark which he handed to Dag.

"Here, little hare, look at it well. This is the soul of Niels Goat and of many a man and woman. They make of their hearts a purse, and would gladly wear fetters, if they were made of silver."

Dag held the coin in his palm and gazed at it; then he gave it back to Lars. Instead of putting the mark back into his purse, the man handed it to Bodil. She raised it to her mouth and bit on it. This made Black Lars laugh mockingly and she threw the mark back to him.

Black Lars flipped the coin, looked at it, and then —
to their astonishment — hurled it across the field. They
all watched it rise into the air and heard it strike a stone
when it fell. Bodil leapt to her feet; her face looked like
a curse. In the twilight night, the coin would be impos-
sible to find. Black Lars laughed but not heartily; the
silver mark was half his fortune, and he was already re-
gretting having thrown it away to satisfy a whim.

"If you find it, you can keep it," he said. Bodil turned
towards the cart as if she had no interest in the coin.
This time Peter laughed.

"If you are so rich," she said to Lars, "that you can
mock the poor, and feed the trolls of Blekinge with
silver, will you lend me your horse to draw my cart to
Christianopolis?" Bodil's voice trembled and she turned
away while she spoke.

Black Lars glanced across the meadow where the
mare was grazing; even in the dim light, its woeful condition was only too apparent. "Is it a real horse? Or
is it the horse of Hell that grazes in churchyards, when
the owls hoot?" he asked, smiling good-naturedly.

Bodil, who read in his smile that her cart would arrive safely in Christianopolis, asked him whether he
wanted something more to drink. He accepted yet another cup of beer and while he drank it, he described
how he had sat up in a tree, and watched the gamekeeper
and his men beating Niels Goat.

"I almost jumped down to help them. But when I
saw that they were masters at their craft, and knew well

how to do their work, I stayed in my tree because it was safer." Suddenly Lars became grave, "But had they brought their dogs who could have sniffed my hiding place . . ." They all waited but he said no more.

Finally Dag spoke, "Where is Satan?"

"With my wife and daughter."

"And where are your wife and child?" Bodil asked.

"Where anyone who wants to do them harm will not find them easily," he replied.

Dag smiled and thought, 'He does not trust *her*, even though she is his wife's cousin.'

"This sword," Lars patted the weapon affectionately, "I received honestly, for I bought it from a soldier. The musket and the powder horn I have had so long that I have forgotten how I got them . . . As for the horse, I took it for its own sake. That poor dumb animal followed me as if my pockets were filled with oats. I think it was tired of dragging a plow, and has the true spirit of a soldier in its heart. I wouldn't part with it for the crown of Sweden."

Dag looked at the horse. It was a gelding, a beautiful young animal. He wished that Black Lars had not stolen it — not because he cared about the farmer who had owned it, but because it hurt to have to think of Black Lars as a thief.

"Now you are going to Kalmar to join the King?" Peter asked sullenly, for he had begun to realize that Black Lars was a rival both for Dag's esteem and Bodil's heart.

"I'll fight until I get enough to buy some land," Black
Lars replied seriously. "If I had had a farm of my own, I
would never have become a soldier."

Dag rolled over on a stone and woke to find the sun
already risen. He sat up and rubbed his eyes. Kirsten
was lying next to him, and a little further away lay Black
Lars and Peter Gram. He was surprised that Bodil was
not there; but then he caught sight of her on the other
side of the field. She was crawling on all fours looking
for the silver mark. Dag smiled and lay down again.
Black Lars was snoring. 'I hope she never, never finds
it,' the boy thought as he closed his eyes.

CHAPTER SIXTEEN

Christianopolis

IF YOU have traveled far and suffered many hardships during your journey, then the name of your destination will sound sweet to you. You will whisper it to yourself, as if it were a prayer or a sacred word that could cure all suffering. To the trouble that awaits you, once you arrive at your destination, you do not give a thought. Traveling in itself has become the purpose of your life. A loose horseshoe, a night's lodging, a dry cloak, or a warm meal are the only problems worthy of consideration. But once the magic place has been reached, its magic is gone; and awaiting you, like patient ghosts, are all the worries and troubles that you thought you had left behind, when you set out on your journey.

Bodil dreamt of Christianopolis and her dreams sprang from avarice. A hundred times she had calculated how great a price her two barrels of schnapps would fetch; and a hundred times she had counted the coins and held the silver in her hands.

Peter Gram imagined the stronghold to be like the castle of Nyborg, which he had known as a child and where his father had been a trumpeter. While they rested along the way, he had many pleasant daydreams in which he walked beside the King, through halls of splendor. Dag tried to keep his dreams from flying too high. Yet he often mumbled the name, Christianopolis, and because the name of the King was mirrored in the name of the fortress, he expected its towers to be tall and its battlements strong.

Kirsten, the youngest of them, had given the least thought to their destination. Since they had left Frederiks Castle, she had known more happiness than ever before in her short life. She had a heart well built for loving; and though such a heart can know much pain, I count those men and women, who possess such a treasure, richer than any king or queen. Dag filled her days and her thoughts; her only fear was that she might lose him. Once she had had a bird with a broken wing which she had thought was tamed; but when its wing healed, the bird had flown away. Another pet had been a cur: a dog more used to kicks than affection before Kirsten had befriended it. A soldier had shot the dog for the sake of showing his skill with a musket.

The last mile or two before you reach Christianopolis, the land is flat; yet you have no view of either the stronghold or the sea; for great boulders, trees, and bushes hinder your seeing far. The road winds like a river, taking the course with the least obstruction. Prickly brambles, which in late summer are filled with berries, keep the wanderer from straying off the road.

It is a pleasant landscape, and only the gulls in the air tell you that you are not far from the sea.

"The King has taken Christianopolis with him to Kalmar; and we should have gone there, too." Black Lars looked with disgust at a particularly large rock. Dag, who since the man's arrival had followed him like a puppy, ran to the boulder and climbed it.

"Can you see anything?"

The boy shook his head and Black Lars laughed. Peter Gram, who was leading the mare, and had been a little behind the others, now caught up with them. Dag's desertion to Black Lars had hurt the singer, yet he felt that he deserved no better treatment. Peter inhaled a deep breath of air. "I think I can smell the sea." The mare whinnied as if it wanted to say something, too.

The children laughed; but Bodil, who had become more and more impatient, the nearer they came to their goal, walked on alone.

"She smells the soldiers' silver and fears they will spend it before she comes." With the end of the reins, Black Lars hit the rump of the gelding: his soldier's steed which had now become a carthorse.

A few more times the road twisted, without the disappointed travelers being able to see anything but more turns ahead. Finally, when the land became marshy and treeless, they saw the fortress of Christianopolis.

"It has a name too long and difficult to say. Christian's Village would have been better!" Peter Gram's voice was as filled with astonishment as with regret. It

did seem almost unbelievable that a small island, surrounded by a wall of no great height, with low houses,
which did not look much better than hovels, should be
the stronghold and largest supply depot of King Christian's great army.

Black Lars spat on the ground and Bodil looked angrily at the mare, as if that poor animal were at fault.
Kirsten moved away from her mother, for she knew
that Bodil could make her suffer for the absence of
towers and spires at Christianopolis.

They heard the sound of a trumpet. The martial
music coming from the fort awakened their hopes a little
and they walked on.

"We have enough of your kind here. Turn your cart
around and go back where you came from." Jens Bjornson, the Commandant of the fortress, stood on the drawbridge, barring their entrance.

"We are honest tradesmen," Bodil replied. In one
hand she held the reins of her mare, which was again pulling the cart; for Black Lars wanted to enter Christianopolis on his gelding.

"Honest merchants!" the Commandant laughed
sourly. "Thieves you are! Thieves who should be
flogged and put in the stocks."

Bodil's red cheeks showed her anger; but she knew
that it had to be checked, and she kept her voice low
and soft as if she were speaking to a lover. "I am but
a poor woman forced to wander the roads in order to
obtain food for my children. None but my mother has

ever whipped me and the hangman has never branded me." Bodil started to open her bodice, to prove that her body had never been marked by the executioner's iron. "See for yourself, Sir."

The three soldiers who were standing guard started to laugh at the spectacle, and the Commandant blushed, for he had difficulty keeping order among his men.

Black Lars rode forward. "I know her, Sir. She comes from Frederiks Castle, where she has a small shop. She is an honest woman."

Bodil relaced her bodice and bowed her head.

"And who are you?" Jens Bjornson looked at Lars suspiciously, as he tried to decide whether the man was a soldier or merely a robber masquerading as one. Black Lars's clothes were motley, with no two things matching each other, but they were not ragged. His sword was a common type worn without a sheath. His musket was ordinary, too. Only his powderhorn, which had a silver lid, was of superior quality.

"I am a yeoman traveling to Kalmar to join the army of the King." Black Lars gazed frankly at the Commandant. "The King knows me well and sets great value on my skill with a musket." The onetime poacher smiled engagingly; and the Commandant could not help but admire his free and easy manner. Nodding to his guards, he indicated that Bodil's cart might enter.

In truth, they had judged Christianopolis a little too harshly, for the fort, which was not yet finished, was well conceived.

Christianopolis is an island which lies in an east-west position. It is long and slender and shaped like the needle of a compass. Its eastern tip is so close to the mainland that a drawbridge connects them. Here the fortress has its highest bastion and it is armed with cannons. In the west the island becomes very low; therefore, the wall which surrounds the fort cuts across the island at this point, leaving the western tip to its original inhabitants: the gulls.

Once inside the fortress, you might think — while walking along either of its two streets — that you were in a small town. There are not only houses for storage, but dwelling places for the permanent staff, the petty officers, and some of the soldiers, as well as the workshops of the artisans. In the center of the fortress there is a square and on it there is a church; then, it had no tower. Since that time King Christian has enlarged it, and many a town of no small size would be proud of possessing so beautiful a church.

In the western part of the island, near the wall which separates the fortress from the land of the gulls, there is a large open space. Here stands the only house on the island which has two stories. It is the Commandant's dwelling. In the large field which surrounds it, visitors to the fortress — merchants and their like — are allowed to camp. Wishing to take advantage of its shelter, Bodil chose a spot next to the wall.

"There aren't many soldiers here," Dag said to Kirsten. The children had escaped from the grownups in order to explore the fortress. They had found their way down to the southern shore, which faces the open sea and where there is a wharf.

"Would you like to become a soldier like Lars?" Kirsten asked.

"I'm too young to be a soldier," he replied casually. He was watching a small boat that was sailing towards the wharf. "But maybe when I grow up, I will." The two men in the boat were hauling down their grey, patched sail.

"I'm glad you're too young," the girl said and then added thoughtfully, "I won't marry a soldier."

Still staring at the boat, he said, "Maybe I'll become a sailor."

Kirsten wrinkled her brow; she had been so frightened when they had sailed across the Sound. "I don't think I'd like to marry a sailor, either."

Dag laughed. Kirsten looked at him pensively, then in order to please him, she laughed, too.

The children left the wharf, as soon as the boat was in, and made their way to the square in the middle of the fort. This was the meeting place and sometimes the marketplace of Christianopolis. Kirsten was looking at the church. "It's not at all like the one in Frederiks Castle," she commented, but she did not seem disappointed.

"Who are you?" a child's voice called.

Kirsten and Dag turned around. The boy who had spoken was about ten years old and well dressed. Dag's attention was caught by the sword the boy was wearing. It was a real sword but made to fit a child's hand.

Dag glanced at Kirsten; what was he to say? He stood motionless. "I am Dag of King's Acre," he finally answered, though he felt as if he were telling a lie.

The other boy eyed him haughtily. "My father is the Commandant of Christianopolis and all the children here have to obey me. Kneel when you speak to me."

Uneasily, Dag looked about the square. Nearby a group of soldiers were watching him and grinning. He glanced once more at the boy. 'He *is* the Commandant's son,' he thought. And though he felt sure that in a fair fight he could have beaten him, he knelt. The soldiers laughed and Dag's face flushed.

"Remember to obey me." The boy's voice was thin and had that particularly unpleasant peevish tone of most spoiled children. "You can rise."

Dag stood up. He was furious with himself for having obeyed.

"You may kiss my hand." The boy held out a thin and delicate hand that resembled a girl's; on his third finger he wore a silver ring. Dag wanted to spit at it but all he dared to do was shake his head. The other boy lifted one eyebrow quizzically, a trick which he had learned from his father to express displeasure, but he dropped his hand to his side.

"Knud Bjornson!" a woman, who had just entered the square, called sharply.

"Bow," Knud commanded.

Dag looked at the soldiers and then bowed so low that it was a mockery; and this time the soldiers' laughter was turned against the Commandant's son.

The boy's cheeks grew red and his hand touched the hilt of his sword. Now the woman was crossing the square, scowling as she came. "I'm coming," he muttered, and ran to meet her.

"*Verdammt*, little boy, you should have bloodied his nose," a voice said in a language the children did not understand.

Dag turned around and recognized the Scottish Captain. "*Mutter . . . Mutter . . . Deine mutter . . .*" the man said, laughing as he spoke.

Dag shrugged his shoulders and smiled foolishly; he had not understood. But Kirsten nodded and pointed towards the open field where Bodil's cart was to be found.

The Scotsman stroked his red beard; then he bent down and patted Kirsten on the head. She drew away and hid behind Dag.

"*Ach . . . kinder . . .*" It grieved him that she seemed frightened of him and for a moment, he wished he were back in Scotland. "A child in a war is like a wee mouse living in the house of a cat."

As they left the square, Kirsten said with pride, "I didn't let him touch me."

"He only meant to be kind," Dag said.

Kirsten shook her head vigorously. Dag was still thinking about the boy with the sword. "Would you like to marry the son of the Commandant?" he asked.

Kirsten flung back her head, "I'll only marry you," she said so seriously that Dag took her hand. The girl flushed happily and brought the hand to her lips. Dag tried to pull his hand away, but he did not escape the kiss.

"What if I became a soldier?" he asked teasingly.

Kirsten's eyes filled with tears, "I'll marry you anyway."

CHAPTER SEVENTEEN

The Soldiers Leave

Tᴀᴋᴇ ᴍᴇ with you to Kalmar. We'll use your horse
and you shall have half of everything."

It was early morning and Dag heard the voice as if
it were part of a dream. Bodil's tone was soft and pleading, and the boy knew that she must be talking to Black
Lars. Dag rubbed his eyes; he had been sleeping on some
straw, which was spread out beneath the cart. Kirsten,
who was still asleep, was lying next to him. An old sail
had been draped over the cart to make a tent. Dag lifted
the cloth; Black Lars and Bodil were standing only a few
feet away. It was a beautiful summer day. With a sigh
Dag let the heavy cloth slip back into place, as he lay
down again.

"You can have everything, if you will but keep me
and Kirsten."

Lars replied with a question, "What about the boy?"

Dag now fully awake, listened breathlessly to every
word.

"He's nothing to me," Bodil said carelessly.

Dag was not surprised by Bodil's response; he did not

care what happened to her, either. Still, it made him angry.

"Ay," Black Lars began bitterly, for he was thinking of his own childhood. "The wolves should eat all the little ones who have no parents. The world would be better off and so would they."

Dag had been hoping to hear Black Lars say that he would never go anywhere without him.

"A stray dog cannot pick its own master," Bodil said. "He must be satisfied not to be kicked. But we can take the boy along, if you want him. He's strong — "

"The Swedes are still in Kalmar castle," Black Lars interrupted. "The town itself has probably been burned to the ground. What do you want to go there for?"

"If it's true that half the town is in ashes, then the prices are high. I can sell my mare to the Commissary; he is willing to pay me in wares. I shall buy you the finest sword in Kalmar and a plumed hat, if you want one."

Lars laughed. "Hasn't the silver in your purse bred and multiplied while we have been in Christianopolis?" The promise of a sword and a plumed hat convinced him that Bodil would eventually treat him as she did Peter Gram. 'She pretends to like only men who can master her,' he thought. 'But she will try to break every one of them, as if we were not men but horses.'

Lars may have been wrong; for if Bodil cared for anyone, it was he. But this could not alter that she had moved her figures carelessly on the chessboard, and had lost the game — though she, herself, still did not know it. Softly, caressingly, she whispered, "We would be rich." How could she — who equated kindness with weakness, and generosity with foolishness — have guessed that Black Lars wanted to be respected, even more than he wanted to be rich? He had become a thief and a poacher; but he had been made them by circumstance, not nature. And what he had hated most about his life as a fugitive, was that it had kept him from the company of his fellowman.

"Yes, we would be rich and you would buy me a cocked hat and a sword, so I could play soldier."

"I would buy you anything you wanted." Bodil was trying desperately to please Black Lars; but she did not realize that weakness in a woman was far more attractive to him than strength. For a moment his expression remained unchanged, then he started to laugh.

"Go away!" she said furiously.

"I am not a child who you can send away when it pleases you." Black Lars's voice was deep, as if he spoke from the strong muscles of his body.

Dag did not want to hear any more. He shook Kirsten to awaken her, and lifted his finger to his mouth to warn her to be quiet. The children silently crawled out from under the cart, on the side opposite from Bodil and Black Lars.

When they reached the street, Kirsten said eagerly, "Let's go to the bakery."

"Not today," Dag replied. The ovens which baked bread for the army were now lighted only twice a week, for there were no more than two hundred men at Christianopolis. Most of them were not soldiers. They were old men and invalids, who worked in the fort making shoes, repairing weapons and wagons, or doing any of the dozens of other tasks that are necessary to supply an army.

The children passed the blacksmith's shop. They looked in; only the apprentices were there. They were making nails, their usual occupation when there was no other work to be done. For a few minutes the children stood watching them, but they did not try to beg, for Dag and Kirsten knew that the apprentices — like themselves — were always hungry.

"Let's go to the square and find Red Beard," Dag suggested. "The early service will be over soon."

The Scots Captain attended church every day and said his prayers before he went to sleep; he believed that if a man did not do these things, the Lord might strike him down when next he went into battle. He had retained the faith of his childhood: a belief in a God who was both merciful and vindictive. While Master Jacobeus preached, the Scot dozed, for he understood almost nothing of what the minister said; but when the congregation sang the hymns, he hummed in his booming voice with great vigor.

The square was filled with people when Dag and Kirsten arrived, and to their surprise the doors of the church were closed. Dag heard someone say that the war was over and that King Charles of Sweden was dead.

"Then all of Sweden is ours!" a toothless old man said and waved his arms in the air.

"Haven't we fought hard enough for it!" another man cried jubilantly.

Dag looked about him. Many of the men were maimed and all of them were poor. War had brought them little, and yet they spoke with disdain of peasants and fishermen. Near the boy someone was boasting of his bravery, and the riches he had received, in the Seven Years' War against the Swedes. Dag turned around to look at the man's face; it was old and wrinkled, yet his eyes sparkled when he spoke of plunder.

"There's Peter!" Kirsten exclaimed. The children had not seen the singer since the day before.

Peter approached them slowly, as if there were no one else in the square and nothing of importance would ever happen. In response to the girl's questions he replied casually, "A messenger came from Kalmar while the early service was still going on. The Commandant and some of the officers are in there now." He pointed towards the church.

At that moment the portal opened, and the Commandant followed by a group of officers walked out of the church. Their stern faces revealed that the news from Kalmar had not been of victory. Within a few minutes, everyone in the square knew that there was a battle going on in the streets of Kalmar, and that the Danish Army was hard pressed. All the men who could be spared at Christianopolis were to arm and march north immediately.

As soon as they dared the children ran up to the Scots Captain. At a distance Peter Gram followed them.

"*Verdammt* Swedes! They are dogs you cannot beat sense into . . . You must shoot them!" He smiled at Dag and Kirsten, who turned around pleadingly to Peter. Reluctantly, the singer translated from the red-bearded man's broken German into Danish.

"This land so poor. Better leave it to the wolves and the bears. Ach! it is a bad war!" The Scot was voicing the sentiments of many of King Christian's mercenaries, who found it senseless to fight a war among people so impoverished.

"If I were the son of a great lord, I would not be be here," Peter Gram said.

"*Ach, ja!* I am very foolish," the Scot answered seriously. He had told his lies so often that they were the only truth he knew. The great castle on the moors was far more real in his mind than his true inheritance: a shepherd's crook and a sheepdog past its prime.

All around them people were talking excitedly. Dag heard a man curse war; to the child's amazement, it was the same old soldier who had a few minutes before grumbled at the prospect of peace. Soon Red Beard was surrounded by his men, and Dag and Kirsten were forced to the fringe of the crowd. But none of the soldiers was as tall as the Scots officer; so the children still could see his face with its lively expressions of bewilderment, anger, annoyance, encouragement, agreement, and disagreement, as he tried to answer questions, many of which he hadn't even understood. His deep voice could easily be heard as he *"Verdammt"* first one thing and then another.

"Ach, der kinder . . ." he called to Dag and Kirsten; smiled sadly and waved to them.

Suddenly Black Lars appeared. He was breathless and he glanced about the square wildly, looking for a familiar face.

Kirsten pulled at Dag's arm. "Let's go somewhere else," she said.

Dag did not answer. He was staring at Black Lars, who had found Peter Gram. Lars's sun-browned face shone with elation, as the singer told him of the plight of the Danish Army at Kalmar, for that very desperation gave life to his hope, that he could do great deeds, which would be told about and rewarded.

"Tomorrow, Christ willing, we shall be in Kalmar. Aren't you coming?" Black Lars looked at Peter. He was as gay as if he were inviting the singer to attend a village fair with him.

Peter turned his head away. "I would come, if I had a horse," he mumbled; while to himself, he silently asked a question: 'Am I afraid? Do I stay behind because I am a coward?'

"Come," Kirsten whispered to Dag.

Black Lars had finally noticed the children; he nodded to them but nothing more. He and Peter were now among the men talking to the Scots Captain. Reluctantly, Dag followed Kirsten. Before they left the square, he turned back, Black Lars was laughing. Al-

though the boy knew that the idea was foolish, he felt
that Lars was laughing at him.

"Let's go and see if the ships have come," Kirsten
suggested. For a long time, it had been expected that
reinforcements would arrive from Copenhagen. One
of the soldiers had told the children, that he was sure,
that the Commandant would give a copper coin to the
first person who sighted the fleet.

"There's nothing," Dag said as he looked out over
the calm sea. He glanced at the three small sailing sloops
which were moored at the wharf; the water was too
shallow for larger ships, which had to cast anchor almost
a cannon shot from shore. Suddenly Dag noticed that
among a group of children, who were fishing from the
wharf, was the Commandant's son. Dag did not want
to encounter Knud again, so he turned to Kirsten and
whispered, "Come . . . before he sees me."

But it was too late; the boy had already noticed
Dag and Kirsten, and was walking towards them. "Stop,
I have something to say to you!" he shouted.

Dag turned around just as the other boy was wrin-
kling his nose and sticking out his tongue at Kirsten.
The girl stepped behind Dag for protection.

"My father is going to have all the beggars whipped
out of Christianopolis," he announced and grinned.
"Master Jacobeus says it's not Christian but my father
doesn't care what he says, because Master Jacobeus is
a drunkard. And my father is going to tell the King to
send another minister to the fort."

Dag knew that what the Commandant's son said was
true. Master Jacobeus did drink a great deal and so
did his wife. Yet Master Jacobeus was liked by the
ordinary soldiers and the common people who lived in
the fortress, for they found it easy to forgive a weakness
which they possessed themselves.

"You smell, you're dirty!" Knud spread his nostrils
and sniffed rapidly. Two of the boys behind him im-
itated him, and they all started to laugh.

"Pigs! Pigs!" they screamed.

Kirsten was crying. Dag stood silently watching
the laughing faces, while he thought — as he had on
the other occasion when he had been taunted by the
Commandant's son — 'I could beat him in a fair fight.'

Still laughing, the Commandant's son and the other
children returned to their fishing. Dag spat after them.
But spitting did not console him any more than the
thought of fighting Knud Bjornson had quieted his
anger. It was the first time that Dag had experienced
that terrible humiliation, which a strong man feels when
he has to bend and bow to weakness, merely because it
is wearing a lace collar. Some people — and Dag was
one of them — seem to be born with a free spirit. Such
is the strange nature of man that from a hen's egg is
sometimes hatched a bird with wings that can soar, and
in the eagle's nest one finds a brood of chickens.

"I wish that Bodil would give him a whipping," Kirsten said with so much determination that Dag smiled,
and his fury was gone.

"He is a coward," he said. Then he added, "I'll bet

he's afraid of the dark and wouldn't dare go out alone at night. I'm sure he's afraid of witches and trolls."

"I'm afraid of witches and I'm very afraid of trolls," Kirsten confessed solemnly. "Witches are just bad human beings but trolls are like devils, and they can eat children up."

"I think witches are worse," Dag disagreed. "A troll lives near our pond. Many people have seen it, but it never did anyone any harm. One night it rode our mare. We found her in the morning trembling and covered with sweat, but she didn't die from it."

Slowly the children returned to the cart. In the same merry spirit which he had shown in the square, Black Lars was preparing to leave.

King Christian had believed when he chose the island that nature had provided him with a perfect fortress, which even a small garrison could defend. Once the drawbridge was up, it was truly surrounded by water instead of by a mere moat. His messenger from Kalmar had said that the King needed as many soldiers as could be spared at Christianopolis; nonetheless, Jens Bjornson may have been too zealous in his interpretation of his master's order, for he kept at the fort only enough soldiers to guard the drawbridge. Still, it was not a large number that set out that afternoon for Kalmar: twelve men on horseback and fifty foot soldiers.

Almost everyone had gathered to watch them leave, yet no one cheered when the red-bearded Scot flourished his plumed hat. A few of the onlookers waved and wished them Godspeed; but the crowd was downcast as if they had only now realized, how few able soldiers there had been at Christianopolis. Peter Gram was probably the only person among the spectators who was glad to see the soldiers depart, for their leaving finally resolved his dilemma of whether he ought to be among them.

Dag and Kirsten had climbed to the top of the bastion above the drawbridge. When the girl spied Black Lars among the horsemen, she called his name; and he lifted his cap into the air and smiled. At first Dag thought of not responding; but then he felt ashamed, and waved with both his hands.

Bodil had remained behind at her cart. Her parting word to Black Lars had been that he was a fool. She was hurt; and truly, she did not understand why he preferred to risk his life for wealth rather than to acquire it as an "honest tradesman." But she cursed him because he had taken the gelding, which she had come to regard as her own property.

That evening the sunset was particularly beautiful. As the sun disappeared, the sky became dark red and a light breeze began to blow from the east.

CHAPTER EIGHTEEN

St. Hans' Eve

MOST PEOPLE do not know the day on which they were born. In some families children arrive as quickly as do the years. When there are six or seven children to be fed and as many asleep in the churchyard, how can one recall the date of every child's birth? Among those who can afford it, the Name Days are still celebrated, in spite of the bishops' protests that they are no different from Saints' Days; and therefore, a Popish custom. Bishops can command but they are not always obeyed. The Name Days are printed in the almanac, and a man need only be able to spell his own name, to discover which day is his. Dag was the exception; he not only knew the date of his birth; but he had been his parents' only child, so they had made much of that day. Besides, he had been born on St. Hans' Eve, the longest day of the year, when the sun tarries beneath the horizon but a few hours.

When Dag awoke in the morning on the twenty-third day of June, in the year of Our Lord, 1611, he said to himself, "I am eight years old." As the day had drawn closer, more and more often, the boy had thought of the summer before, when his mother and father had been alive.

He looked about him; Kirsten had risen already. "I'm still Dag of King's Acre," he whispered; but burning tears filled his eyes. 'I'll tell no one that it's my birthday . . . Kirsten knows but I'll command her to be silent . . . Bodil doesn't care whether I'm eight or eighty . . .' Suddenly Dag thought of Peter Gram. Hadn't he told the singer that his name was Dag because he was born on St. Hans' Eve? Black Lars knew it; but Black Lars had been gone for two days. Dag stretched himself and rubbed his eyes. He tried not to think about Black Lars because he missed him.

He pushed aside the cloth and crawled out from under the cart. Sleep still clung to his body. He tried to comb his hair with his hands but it was too dirty. Then he decided to go to the lower part of the island in order to bathe. He had started towards the door in the corner of the wall, when he heard Peter call him. The boy turned around and looked with contempt at the singer, as — with a child's intolerance — he compared him to Black Lars. The gangling young man, who never seemed to know why he did things, and was ordered about by Bodil, and laughed at by other men, was seen by Dag in unhappy contrast to the brave soldier riding boldly to Kalmar.

"Here." Peter handed the child a slice of bread and a piece of cold fried fish.

Dag sat down on the ground across from the singer and started to eat, without thanking him.

The man was staring at the boy. He knew only too well what the child thought, and he all but shared his disgust. Ever since Black Lars had joined them, Peter had tried to find the flaws in his character, so that he might hate him. But Peter did not know how to hate, and so he was forced to confess that Black Lars deserved the child's admiration.

"Kirsten told me that it is your birthday. May God grant you many more," Peter said shyly.

Dag did not even look up, as he told himself that he would punish Kirsten for telling his "secret" to Peter.

"The longest day of the year . . . and the shortest night . . . St. Hans' Eve . . ." Peter continued good-naturedly.

Again Dag remembered the year before: how happy he had been on that birthday; how his father had given him a knife. Then he recalled — as he had so often and with the same sadness — that he had lost the knife. His father had scolded him; but this memory was not as bitter as Dag's belief, that the losing of the knife had been an omen of the terrible events, that were to happen the following year.

"It is a magic night," Peter said and smiled. "Do you know where Bodil is . . ."

"I don't think she slept here last night," Dag replied. To the boy, Bodil's absence was always welcome.

"I asked where she was now," Peter argued irritably. "I don't care where she spends her nights."

"I hate her," Dag said.

The singer shook his head slowly. "No, you don't."

In his mind Dag listed the reasons why Bodil deserved his hate; and then he understood that Peter Gram was right. He did not care about Bodil, not even enough to hate her. "But sometimes . . . when she hits Kirsten, I could . . . I could . . ." He stopped speaking. The world was filled with grownups who beat children, to hate Bodil for this reason seemed silly. 'But I hate the Commandant's son,' Dag thought. 'Him I truly hate.'

"She's sold the mare to the Commissary, hasn't she?" Peter asked.

Dag shrugged his shoulders. "It could never pull the cart again." Slowly he stood up and started to walk away. Peter was going to say something, and the boy feared that he knew what it would be: Peter would remind him of how much he had once cared, what happened to the mare. And Dag knew that he would not be able to explain to Peter, how he could still be fond of the animal, without thinking it wrong that it be sold for slaughter.

"I'm going to the beach to bathe," Dag mumbled so softly that he was not sure that the singer had heard him; then he ran towards the door that lead to the meadow.

"The Land of the Gulls" — as the little field that pointed like an arrow towards the west was called — being outside the fortress, was a favorite place for the children of Christianopolis to play. The night before it had rained; the grass was very green and filled with the flowers of early summer. Some sheep and three horses were grazing there; they moved away as Dag approached. The boy stood still; and then, very cautiously with his hand turned palm up, he tried to get near one of the horses; but the animal was frightened and began to gallop in the opposite direction.

On the northern shore there was a small bay with a sandy beach. No one was there, and the boy was glad; for Dag had much of his father in him and he liked to be alone.

While he undressed, he thought about Peter Gram. When they had first met, Peter had called him his little brother; and he had been pleased. But why was the singer so like a child? Why did he do everything that Bodil commanded? They were both grownups and he was stronger than she; then Dag thought of the Commandant's son and how he had obeyed him. "No, it is not the same," he murmured. "Black Lars only laughed at Bodil."

The sun was warm on his back, but when he dipped his toe into the water, it felt cold. Lightly, he kicked the water, and little waves moved in semicircles away from the shore. Suddenly he recalled how Black Lars and his wife had talked to each other in the grave chamber. "Maybe," he whispered, "nobody cares for anybody."

The boy sat down in the water and splashed his feet. Across from him was the mainland. A heron took flight from among the reeds that grew along the edge

of the water. He watched the long, slow movements
of its wings, as it flew towards him. But suddenly it
veered and he could see it no more: it must have landed
on one of the little islands in the large bay. He wondered how deep the water was, and if one might walk
to the mainland by following the chain of tiny islands.

"Dag!"

He recognized Kirsten's high, thin voice, and guessed
by her tone that she had already seen him. He made
no attempt to hide, but he turned over onto his stomach
and moved a little further out into the water.

"Where have you been?" he asked.

"The Commandant's son is gone!" she exclaimed. "I
saw them. He and his mother were sitting in a wagon
drawn by two horses, and there were soldiers, one on
each side of the wagon."

"What does it matter to me what happens to the
Commandant's son?" Dag said, but he was surprised by
the bitterness of his own voice. Then he asked himself
silently, 'Why should I care, except to be glad because
I won't have to see him again?' And finally, he did
smile for the promise that he would not be humiliated
again by Knud Bjornson did make Christianopolis a
much pleasanter place.

Kirsten sat down on the sand next to Dag's little pile
of clothes.

"You haven't told me where you've been," Dag remarked.

"Peter sent me to look for Bodil."

"Did you find her?" the boy asked.

The girl dug her fingers into the sand. "No," she said without looking up.

'She's lying,' Dag thought. 'She did find her.' But he said nothing for he did not care what Bodil did; but to Kirsten it could not help but matter, and he felt pity for the girl. Balancing himself on one hand, he sprayed water at her with the other.

Kirsten picked up his clothes and covered herself with them. Dag laughed, filled his mouth with water, and spat it in her direction. "The water's warm," he said.

The girl stood up and smiled, then she stripped herself of her rags. She did not go in the water right away; but, as Dag had done, stood at the edge and stuck in a toe to test the warmth. Dag looked at her feet and noticed how filthy they were. He raised his head and gazed at her. Now that she was naked he realized how thin she was. 'And yet,' he thought, 'she's strong for a girl who's only six.'

Dag jumped up and started to throw water at her. Kirsten squealed as it touched her sun-warmed skin. For a moment she was undecided, should she seek the safety of the shore or splash back?

She threw herself in the water, then with her legs she kicked it into a tumult. They screamed and splashed each other until Dag was breathless and ran up upon the beach.

He lay down on the sand and Kirsten sat down across from him. "She was with the Commissary, the one who bought the mare."

"I knew you were lying," Dag said, as he filled one

hand with sand and let it slowly sift into the other. "Why did you lie?"

"I don't know. Maybe because I am bad . . . Sometimes I lie just to be bad." Kirsten was gazing at the walls of the fort.

"I know what you mean," Dag agreed. A lie was something you could hide in. "Peter lies all the time," he added as he formed a little hill of sand and planted a twig on top of it.

"Why?" Kirsten asked.

"I don't know . . ." Slowly he started to dig, undermining the twig on the top of the cone of sand until it fell. "I don't understand grownups."

"Look." Kirsten pointed to the hole she had dug; an ant was caught in it. The ant tried to climb the sides but the dry sand gave way under its tiny feet. At once it started all over again; this time it almost reached the top, when the sand became a miniature avalance and sent it tumbling down. Dag let a thin stream of sand flow onto the ant and it disappeared. A moment later it pushed its head up from beneath the little mound, and without hesitation attacked the sides of the hole. This time it, finally, climbed over the edge and scurried away towards the meadow.

"It wasn't just to lie," Kirsten said and hid her face in her folded arms. "She is my mother and she's always with the soldiers! I hate her! I don't want her to be with the soldiers! . . . She's my mother!"

Dag listened to Kirsten cry; he did not know what to say. He formed another little hill; then in anger, he destroyed it. "She's not your mother. You're a princess. Remember, you told me that your mother was a queen."

The girl looked up at him; her tears were mixed with sand. "No, I know that Bodil is my mother! That was just . . . It was just a lie."

Dag wanted to tell Kirsten that it was not a lie, that a lie was something different; and although he was certain that he was right, he could not find the words to explain it.

They lay on the sand for a while without speaking; and then, as if they had both gotten the idea at the same time, they rose and put on their clothes. As they crossed the meadow, Kirsten took Dag's hand in hers and he let her keep it.

CHAPTER NINETEEN

The Commandant

JENS BJORNSON, the Commandant of Christianopolis, had been down at the wharf peering anxiously out over the sea. He felt uneasy. The ships with men and supplies should have arrived a week before, and still not a sail was to be seen. Had he been a man worthy of his position, he would have refused the King's appeal and sent no soldiers to Kalmar; but he had only the desire to rule, not the ability. Because he was torn by doubt, even when he issued an unimportant order, the cleverest and least scrupulous of the men under his command, commanded him.

Today all work had stopped within the fortress at noon, without his permission; and everywhere were signs of preparation for the celebration of Midsummer. Jens Bjornson was not stupid; he knew that in an undermanned fort, liquor should be forbidden and the most rigid discipline enforced. Yet when he had demanded an explanation from the Sergeant-at-Arms, he had let himself momentarily be persuaded that the men might mutiny, if they were not allowed to celebrate St.

Hans' Eve. He knew that by midnight he, himself, would be the only sober man on the island; and yet all he had done, to try to prevent a drunken revelry, was to ask the Sergeant to give his word that he would not drink: a promise which the Commandant knew he would not keep.

As he passed a row of low wooden sheds where supplies were kept, he saw the Sergeant-at-Arms. One glance at the man's ruddy face proved how futile it had been to believe in, or be convinced by, anything he said. The Sergeant, who was accompanied by Bodil and the Commissary, had already been drinking.

Bodil curtsied, and the men removed their caps and bowed. The Commandant blushed from both anger and shame. When he was a few steps beyond them, they started to giggle; and he felt sure that they were laughing at him.

When he arrived at the gate, he found only two soldiers on guard duty and the drawbridge down. He had issued an order, as soon as the men had departed for Kalmar, that the drawbridge was not to be lowered without his permission. Now he helped the two soldiers hoist the drawbridge, and repeated his former order as if it were a new one. The men bowed but they also grinned and he had to check his temper; his hand was on his sword's hilt, and what he wanted to do was to hit them with the flat side of his sword. 'Not now,' he cautioned himself, 'it is too late now to enforce obedience by beating. I'll remember their faces and send them to Kalmar as soon as reinforcements come.'

When he returned to his house, the fires, that had been built near the western wall, were lighted. He had noticed them being stacked earlier, but he felt that it was an insult that they should be set ablaze now, when he could watch it being done. 'I must talk to Master Jacobeus,' he thought angrily.

It was characteristic of Jens Bjornson that the moment he had determind upon an action, something within him pressed him to do the opposite. "I don't want to talk with him," he said to himself as his legs carried him to the portal of the church.

Master Jacobeus, who was not sober, had seen the Commandant rushing across the square, and went out to meet him. "Christ be with you!" he called gaily from a distance. The general spirit of the day had convinced him that an extra bottle of wine at the midday meal would not be amiss; and the minister had only friendliness for everyone, even the Commandant, whom he did not like. "It's going to be a beautiful evening." He threw out his arms as if he wished to embrace all of Christianopolis, if not the world.

The Commandant, who feared that the minister was about to put his arms around him, halted. "There is not a sober man in the fort!" he fumed.

Master Jacobeus gazed shamefacedly at the ground. Although he was a drunkard, he was the first to confess that drinking was a vice. Long ago he had learned that this was the best weapon against censure. When anyone expressed disapproval of his behavior, he immediately condemned himself to one of the lowest pits in

Hell; and often, in order to stop his flow of words, his adversary would begin to console him.

"What are all the fires for?" Jens Bjornson asked, as though he thought that the minister had built them.

"The fires?" he replied with pretended innocence. "They are always lighting fires for one thing or another." The Commandant continued to stare at him quizzically and Master Jacobeus, who had accepted a drink from Bodil that morning, pursed his lips and said, "They are going to roast a couple of sheep, I believe."

"Whose sheep?" the Commandant snapped.

The minister flung his arms upwards and shook his head to indicate his ignorance. With amazement, he noticed that Jens Bjornson had his hand on the hilt of his sword; and Master Jacobeus feared he was going to draw it. "I believe that the Sergeant has bought the sheep," he said and tried not to grin, for everyone knew that the Sergeant never bought anything, but treated the King's property as if it were his own.

Jens Bjornson flushed. First his neck grew red, then slowly the color of his face changed and the vein in his forehead began to throb. He said no more to Master Jacobeus. As he turned on his heel, he decided that he would talk with the people who were preparing the festivities. But in order to reach the western wall, he had to pass his own home, and he went no further.

As he entered his house, his anger subsided but not his irritation with himself. He had long known that the Sergeant-at-Arms was a scoundrel; no better — if not much worse — than a thief. Why hadn't he rid himself of him? "It would have involved a risk," he whispered to himself; "the Sergeant might spread rumors when he got to Kalmar. Better to keep him here and keep an eye on him." This had been his excuse since he had first realized how irresponsible the Sergeant was. And yet what could the man say? What stories could he tell? The Commandant knew that he had never done anything that could be the cause of formal charges being made against him. "There are a lot of wastrels around the King who would like to be Commandant of Christianopolis." He concluded with the same phrase that he had dozens of times before.

Jens Bjornson glanced towards the stairs which led to the three upstairs rooms. He wondered where his wife and his son were. "Hedvig!" he called; and when no one answered, he repeated it louder, "Hedvig!" Only then did he remember that he had sent his wife and child to Lund that very morning. It had been arranged on the spur of the moment. A wagon of supplies had arrived from Lund, with a few horsemen who were to accompany it back. He had filled the wagon with some of their furniture and their more valuable clothing.

He walked into the other room. It was almost bare. His best chair and the inlaid chess table were gone. The Commandant approached the mirror that hung above the fireplace and studied his own face. He made a grimace and then sat down on the broad windowsill. Where were the maid and the cook? Behind the house was a lean-to where the food was made; but why go out there, when he knew for certain that his servants were to be found, where everyone else was: celebrating St. Hans' Eve in the middle of the afternoon.

The house was empty. He would get no supper that night. Despair overcame him and he covered his face with his hands. He was weary and his wife and son were gone. Suddenly tears came into his eyes and rolled down his fingers, onto the backs of his hands. He cried silently until there were no tears left.

CHAPTER TWENTY

The Lute

THE SMELL of the roasting sheep was pleasant to the nostrils of the hungry people gathered around the fires. To the older soldiers it brought back memories of the campaigns of their youth, when they had believed that their swords would bring them fame and riches. Now they had been taught the lessons of the edge and the point of the sword, and knew that when age made them unable to work, begging would become their profession. But for the moment, this was forgotten; and dreams mixed well with reality, as they drank from the stoneware jugs.

The men sat closest to the fires; the women behind them; on the fringe of each circle were children. Dag and Kirsten sat on a large rock by themselves; they had made no friends among the other children. Kirsten had at last spied her mother. Bodil was the only woman sitting near the largest of the fires. On her right was the Sergeant-at-Arms and on her left, the Commissary.

The office of Commissary is the most despicable in any army. Everyone believes the Commissary to be a thief; and often as not, this is true. Since there is no honor attached to the work of supplying the army, a nobleman will never seek it, and it is seldom held by a man from a respectable family. It is left for the common people: to corporals and sergeants who are clever and ambitious; and they are willing to fight over it. Many a Commissary has been executed and many murdered on a dark night by hungry soldiers; but more than a few have retired from service wealthy enough to buy a large farm, or become a merchant with a pew in church; and more than one has been awarded a coat of arms.

The Commissary began to sing; but he had no voice, so he shouted. Dag thought of Peter. He was nowhere to be seen. The boy regretted that he had been so unfriendly to the singer that morning. Anger against Peter Gram often overwhelmed Dag; but it was always momentary and left him with the feeling that he had caused the singer undeserved pain. What Dag could not forgive in Peter was that he was foolish; and yet the boy knew that foolishness did not stem from evil.

He turned to Kirsten and said that he was going to find the singer. "I have to talk with him about something," he remarked with embarrassment. He jumped down from the rock and walked away without looking back, so as not encourage Kirsten to follow him.

When he entered the street, he tried to whistle; he had only just learned how and sometimes he didn't succeed in making any sound at all. 'I have to hold my lips correctly,' he thought. Then he wondered whether

Peter really did know how to play the trumpet and could teach him to do it; or if that, too, was one of his lies.

Dag found Peter sitting on the wharf, leaning his back against the fortress wall. The singer was looking at the sea that had borrowed its color from the sunset. Without saying anything, Dag sat down beside him; and Peter nodded as if he were replying affirmatively to a question.

Kirsten, who had been following Dag, thought that now she might "catch up" with him. She cared so terribly whether she displeased Dag; yet the only thing she did repeatedly, which he found irksome, was the one thing she could not keep herself from doing: she would be with him, whether he wanted her nor not.

"Why are we here?" The singer finally spoke.

Dag was bewildered, "Do you mean why we are in Christianopolis?"

"I prayed last night that I should die," Peter said. "A star in the sky blinked twice and I grew so frightened that I prayed to live."

Dag looked at the singer; then he said very firmly, "It is a sin to pray like that."

Peter smiled. "What you say is true; and yet . . . Our pilgrimage seems too long and filled with suffering."

The boy was thinking of the previous winter, of the hunger and cold, and yet he could not remember ever wanting to die.

"I have often prayed that I should die." Kirsten

spoke so gravely that both Dag and Peter turned to look at her.

"You must not pray like that. You must not," Dag said crossly.

Hearing his own thoughts expressed by a child filled Peter with shame, as if the sincerity of Kirsten's wish made his own seem a sham.

"I haven't prayed like that in a long time." Kirsten looked pleadingly at Dag. Her eyes were filled with tears. "It was because I thought that it would be nicer to be an angel."

With a sudden feeling of shame, Dag realized that he had not prayed that his parents should become angels. 'My mother must have become one anyway,' he thought. And in the same instant, he knew that he wished she were alive so much, that even the certainty, that she had become an angel, could not console him. It was easier to think about his father; perhaps his father had not become an angel. 'And I don't think I'll become one myself, when I die,' he thought. Dag looked out over the sea.

In the stillness, sweet melancholy came to them, all three; and they felt very close, as they sat silently watching the colors darken and evening come. The western sky was still filled with gold, while the first pale summer stars could be seen in the southeast.

Peter started to sing; he did not have his lute and his voice sounded clearer without accompaniment. At first, he sang softly, as if apologizing for breaking the silence.

It was not a spring or a summer song; but a song of autumn:

> *Sorrowfully the birds do sing,*
> *As leaves fall to the earth.*
> *Clipped by care is summer's wing*
> *Forgotten is summer's mirth.*
> *Youth is short and care is long,*
> *And lovers' songs are brief.*
> *Only the heart is strong,*
> *It holds our world of grief.*
> *Constant as the winter's scorn*
> *Is not the rose but the thorn.*

When Peter had finished singing, he rose and stretched himself. Dag, who was still under the spell of the song and the beauty of the evening, was surprised and disappointed to see Peter get up. 'We could stay like this forever,' he thought; but he said nothing. A moment later he, too, was standing and Kirsten was on her feet beside him. All three of them looked at each other. Peter shrugged his shoulders and they started to walk back to the field.

The sheep had been taken from the spits and the meat was almost gone when they arrived. Greasy faces told where it had disappeared, and laughter that it had been welcome. All of the men were drunk, as were most of the women, and even some of the children. The Sergeant had provided them with a fine feast, or maybe it was the Commissary. It hardly mattered which, for both meat and drink had belonged to the King.

Peter and the children sat down by Bodil's cart. Near the largest of the fires they had seen Bodil with the Commissary; his arm had been around her waist and her head had been on his shoulder. "She isn't even drunk," Peter had whispered bitterly — a remark which confused both Kirsten and Dag, who thought that one of Bodil's few virtues was that she did not drink too much.

Kirsten, who was always watching her mother, was the first to notice her coming towards them. None of them spoke to her, and she disappeared into the cart without saying a word.

When Bodil came out, she was carrying Peter's lute. She stood in front of the singer with her feet spread far apart, and held out the instrument to him. "Play," she ordered.

Peter's hands stretched forward and he was about to take his beloved lute, when he glanced at Dag's face, and saw there the expression of shame that ought to have been on his own. The singer let his hands fall to his sides and said, "No."

Bodil laughed and again commanded him to play. A small crowd of men stood a short distance from the cart, sniggering.

"Play!" This time Bodil screamed and the laughter behind her was louder; the woman became furious for she feared that for once, it might be she who was being laughed at. She held the lute high above her head, and only whispered the word loud enough for Peter to hear it, "Play."

Peter Gram became pale. His hands, that wanted to

save his lute, were trembling; and because he feared that they might prove treacherous, he shoved them beneath his folded legs.

"Fool!" Bodil screamed and with all her strength threw the lute down on the ground, in front of the singer.

Peter gazed at the broken instrument; it could never be repaired. Slowly he rose and looked intently at Bodil. She smiled. Peter lifted his foot and then stamped on what was left of his lute, breaking its fragile wood into hundreds of splinters.

Again some of the soldiers laughed. Bodil was motionless and she was no longer smiling. With his right hand Peter slapped her face as hard as he could.

CHAPTER TWENTY-ONE

Peter's Flight

W HEN PETER GRAM ran away from Bodil, the broken lute, the fire, and the drunken merrymakers, he wanted to run to the end of the world. He rushed down the empty street of the fort and did not stop until he came to the gate. The drawbridge was up and he hurled himself against its heavy planks. One of the soldiers came out of the guard room, and recognizing him, called his name. Peter backed away as if the drunken man were the devil himself; turning around, he started to run back in the direction from which he had come.

Entering the square, he saw Dag near the church. The boy had been looking for him. The sight of the child stopped Peter's wild flight, and he stood trembling like a deer who is surrounded by hunting dogs. Dag looked up at the man and smiled timidly.

Peter turned his face from him. "I'm going away," he mumbled.

"Will you take me with you?" Dag asked.

Peter shook his head.

"I don't know if Bodil will let me stay with her . . .

I heard her say to Black Lars that —" Dag glanced at Peter and when he saw the expression in his eyes, he stopped speaking.

For a moment the singer felt a bitter hatred against Dag. "I'm leaving," he said again, as if the words had a deeper meaning; and he started to walk down the narrow street which led to the wharf.

"I couldn't go without Kirsten, anyway," the boy muttered, not loud enough to be heard by the man who was already several yards away. "It wouldn't be right for me to go away without Kirsten, would it?"

Suddenly Peter Gram stopped and turned around. Dag thought he was coming back.

"God be with you," Peter called.

"God be with you," the boy replied.

Peter waved and the boy waved back; and the man turned again in the direction of the wharf.

The pink of the sunset was moving from west to east. Soon the sun would rise again. The sky was cloudless, and the not too distant shore of the mainland was plainly visible. Peter wondered how deep the water was, for he could not swim. The wharf was deserted. Three small sloops and two rowboats were tied to it. In one of them he found oars.

Peter lowered himself into the rowboat and loosened the moorings. He had never rowed before, and it was more difficult than he had supposed. But there was neither wind nor wave, and soon Peter's boat reached the shallow water near the beach of the mainland. He pulled in the oars and sat staring at the fortress.

Suddenly he noticed that someone was coming through the portal in the wall which led to the wharf. He leapt into the water and looked back: a child was standing on the edge of the wharf, and Peter knew it was Dag. First Peter dragged the boat up onto the beach; then he waved.

'I couldn't have taken him with me,' he thought. 'I don't even know where I am going.'

He was about to call, "Christ be with you," to the boy; but he feared that there might be a sober man in Christianopolis, who would hear him. Peter waved again, this time with both his arms; but the boy did not wave back.

When Peter reached the highland, north of Christianopolis, he gained a view of the fort for the last time. More wood had been thrown on the fires and they were blazing high. He was too far away to hear the noise, but he could see that some of the people were dancing. He spat on the ground, and looked towards the east where the sky was blood-red from the coming sun.

As the forest closed around him, Peter felt as if a miracle were happening to him, as if he had been blind, and now suddenly were being given his sight. He saw how graceful the birch trees were with their long drooping branches and their white, slender trunks; they were like young women combing their hair. And the oak,

gnarled and stiff, its branches unmoved by the winds, was an old man filled with knowledge and stories of bygone times. Peter's eyes saw the birds and his ears heard them; even an old toad that sat in the middle of the path — contemplating both ditches at once with its sad eyes, as if it did not know in which direction to leap — seemed to Peter good and beautiful. He walked with long strides and his legs did not feel the weight of his body. He had shed the past as a snake sheds her skin. He was in the pleasant world of fairy tales: of good and evil. He was in a world of beautiful colors, where darkness and light, like two shining knights, are forever fighting their battles; but the grey world does not exist.

By noon the warmth of the sun, and the fatigue from having walked so far, made him want to rest. He found a place under an old oak tree, where the grass grew high, and he lay down. He caught a glimpse of the sky and saw a white cloud sailing across it. He thought of the past — of how he had once been — and he decided for the hundredth time that day that from now on, everything would be different. With relish he imagined himself as he had been before — and the picture was as true as the woodcuts of the Pope, that you can buy in Copenhagen for a copper coin in which he resembles the devil. If man cannot be good, he likes to think of himself as evil; and vanity does not care, it grows well in either soil. Slowly the blue sky became dark, the boughs of the oak disappeared; and Peter Gram was asleep.

*

The sun had set, it was late in the evening when Peter awoke. At first he did not know where he was; he touched the grass with wonder; then slowly he remembered the broken lute, his flight from the fort, and his long march. But the magic was gone. He sat up; his back ached and he was hungry. In the white night, he could see all the trees clearly but they were only trees. An owl hooted. Peter rubbed his ankles. "It was good I left," he said aloud.

'But you didn't leave, you fled,' a voice within him argued. 'You have always fled, never stood your ground and taken battle.'

It was chilly and he shuddered. 'I should have taken Dag with me.' The thought seemed to have come from nowhere; but when it was phrased, the picture of the boy standing alone on the wharf appeared in his mind like a ghost. 'God meant me to take the boy and then the devil tempted me to go alone.' Self-pity overcame him, he looked at the ground and declared loudly to the lonely forest: "You are a coward, Peter Gram. You are a fool!"

But he had made that confession too many times, and it did not lessen his pain. 'I could go back and get the boy.' He repeated his thought aloud, "I could go back . . ." He smiled. Now he understood clearly that roads do divide, at the crossroad there is a choice, and blinding oneself to it is a form of choosing, too: it is the fool's way, the coward's way.

Peter started back towards the fort. He did not walk

with the same light steps that he had before. Many a time he paused, many a time he called himself a fool; but still he walked on, back to Christianopolis to find the boy, back to his defeat, to claim his victory from it.

CHAPTER TWENTY-TWO

Despair

D AG SAW Peter Gram wave to him from the mainland, but he didn't wave back. A few days ago he had hated him, and had Peter left then, he would have turned his back on him; or maybe even thrown a stone after him to show his contempt. But he no longer hated Peter; in a strange, listless way he loved him. He was glad that the singer had gone, glad that he had escaped; but his happiness was like that of the prisoner, who sees the doors of the dungeon open for his fellow sufferer, but not for himself.

Man does not grow as the blessed grain which shoots up each day, a little higher towards the sun, until in autumn, it is heavy with its own richness and again bends towards the earth. In a day a boy can become a man, and one kiss can turn a girl into a woman. One word can sometimes build a world, and one glance shatter it. You can lie down to sleep, thinking you know who you are, and wake up to find yourself a stranger. Master Luther saw the devil, as Jacob saw the ladder which led

to heaven; and neither of them ever forgot what he had
seen. A vision can change a man, and blight or growth
will follow.

Dag stayed on the wharf long after he had seen Peter
Gram disappear into the forest. He watched the sun
rise. It was going to be a beautiful day. If only Peter
had said, "I'll come back to get you as soon as I've
seen the King"; even if it had been a lie. Suddenly
the boy thought of Black Lars; then he shook his head.
He did not want to remember him either. They were
alike; neither of them could be trusted.

A heron flew over the water, but the boy did not see
it. Behind his eyes despair was building a wall; and for
the first time, he thought that he should have died with
his father and mother. Tears started to form in his eyes
and he did not wipe them away. It was his loneliness
which made him cry; that and the certainty that no
grownup in the world cared about him. It is a truth
that even a grownup's heart finds difficult to bear; and
whose weight he makes lighter by saying, "It is the Will
of God." This escape was not open to Dag, for though
he knew a grownup's despair, he had only a child's
weapons with which to fight it.

"Dag!"

The boy looked away. It was Kirsten and he did not
want to see her.

"Dag," she said again pleadingly.

Dag turned around. She was standing only a few feet
away from him. "Go away!" he said furiously, although
he did not know where his anger had come from.

The girl, who was wondering what she might have done to deserve his wrath, stood still.

"Go away!" Dag shouted, and then he screamed, "I hate you!" The girl turned slowly; but when Dag said a second time that he hated her, she began to run.

To Dag's surprise his tears stopped. He wiped his eyes. 'I'll go to Kalmar myself,' he thought. 'I'll learn to play the trumpet.' But then he thought of Peter and he decided that he did not want to learn to play any instrument. He would go and seek the King. And all the dreams that he had ever had, rode through the boy's brain like mad horsemen. His tears came back; but this time he hid his face in his hands for he was ashamed.

Tears, even from sorrow, eventually dry or there would be no laughter in the world. Dag took his hands away from his face.

The sea which mirrored the small islands, the birds, the warm sun, all became real again. I must look for Kirsten,' he thought. 'How I must have frightened her.'

Dag went first to the open field near the western wall. Many of the soldiers who had taken part in the Midsummer feast had not bothered to return to their quarters, and were sleeping on the grass. Dag lifted the old sail that shaded Bodil's cart. Underneath it, he made out two sleeping figures; he bent down: one of them was Bodil and the other was the Commissary. With disgust he let the canvas fall. It was the grownup world and he had finished with it.

When he reached the square, he found the minister sitting in front of the church; he was still drunk. At

the sight of the child, Master Jacobeus hiccupped,
sniffed, started to cry, and then called him. The boy
stood motionless staring at him, as if he were some kind
of monster. Master Jacobeus who was but a silly fool,
with a sentimental heart and too great a thirst, flushed
and bowed his head. He swore to himself, as he had a
thousand times before, that he would never drink
again.

Everywhere there were signs of complete disorder.
The drawbridge was down and the guards, who were
not sober from the night before, had already started
to drink again. It was as though a kind of madness had
overtaken the island.

Only the Commandant, Jens Bjornson, was not drunk,
but his sobriety was also a form of insanity. He shouted
orders to people who could hardly understand them; and
then walked away, as if he did not care whether they
obeyed him or not.

Even now, had the Commandant collected the few
soldiers who were still capable of carrying out an order,
and with their help arrested the worst offenders, he
might have brought sanity back to the fort. But he only
issued threats against everyone, even the people who
might have helped him. He was like a rider on a run-
away horse, who instead of trying to regain control of
the animal, lets the reins go and hangs onto the horse's
neck.

When Dag returned from the eastern part of the
island and was approaching the field again, he remem-

bered the cove where they had bathed. 'That's where she is!' he thought, and laughed at how foolish he had been not to think of it before. The door in the corner of the wall was closed, but it was not barred.

He walked across the meadow. "Kirsten!" he called.

There was no answer. 'She's hiding,' he thought; then suddenly he grew frightened. "Kirsten!" he cried again and ran towards the beach, startling the few animals that were grazing at the other end of the meadow.

Kirsten was sitting at the edge of the beach with her feet in the water.

"I'm sorry," Dag said loudly and clearly, but the girl did not even turn her face towards him. "I am sorry," he said softly, and sat down not far away from her. For a while they sat silently, watching the little waves Kirsten made by dipping her feet in and out of the water.

"You hate me," she finally said and moved a little further away from Dag.

"No," he murmured. "No, I don't hate you. It was only . . ." But the boy could not explain what he himself did not understand, so he added, meaninglessly, "It was everything." The girl turned to look at him and he could see that she had been crying. "It wasn't you I hated . . . I hated everyone . . ."

Kirsten smiled because this she did understand. "I was going to drown myself, but then I got scared . . ."

Like a crab, the boy moved across the sand until he was next to her. "Peter is gone . . . Black Lars . . . And then I felt so alone. I cared for them and neither of them wanted me . . ."

"I'm glad Peter wouldn't take you with him," she said.

Dag wanted to tell the girl how he had told Peter that he could not go away without her, but he was too embarrassed. "I'm glad I didn't go, too," he mumbled.

Very seriously the girl gazed into his eyes, "Truly?" she asked.

Dag, being a child, wrinkled his brow and thought before he answered. Suddenly, he remembered Peter's face, and then Bodil's when she had broken his lute. "Yes," he replied very slowly. "Truly, I am glad I stayed."

Kirsten sighed. Now Dag was eager to convince her that he was speaking the truth. "We will go away together. We can live in the forest, and I can be a hunter like Black Lars." While he spoke, he wondered whether there might once have lived giants in the forest, on this side of the of the Sound too; and if he might find a king's grave chamber as Lars had.

Kirsten grinned shyly. "I didn't drown myself because I was afraid that if I did I would have to live with mermaids all my life and never see you again."

Dag laughed; and when Kirsten heard his laughter, she laughed, too.

CHAPTER TWENTY-THREE

As the Sun Sets

I AM NOT AFRAID to die, I am not." Jens Bjornson repeated aloud the words he had mumbled so often to himself that day. He found in them an excuse for the state of the fort under his command. If fear of death, or lack of it, is the only measuring rod for judging heroes and cowards, then the Commandant was a hero. Jens Bjornson did not fear death, but better it would have been for Denmark and the King, if a coward had been in command of Christianopolis; for his fears would have ensured that the bastions were guarded.

Jens Bjornson drew his sword and held it up. The rays of the evening sun reflected on its polished blade. Loudly he said again, "I am not afraid of death." No one disagreed with him, for he was alone in the main room of the Commandant's house. A madness within the man took pleasure in the knowledge that the fort was unprotected.

He knelt and held his sword upwards, as though he wanted to show it to Our Lord. "He was afraid of death but I am not." The words of blasphemy had been said loudly and defiantly.

The silence that followed frightened Jens Bjornson. He lowered his sword and placed it on the floor in front of him.

A shadow cast by the wooden beam that separated the two windows, slowly grew as the sun set, stretching itself across the floor until it reached the Commandant's sword. Jens Bjornson watched it with horror, as if it were the claw of the devil. Then with wonder he whispered, "It is an omen. It is a sign." He glanced up towards the ceiling, and then down at his sword and the shadow, which together formed a perfect cross.

To Bodil, the Midsummer feast had been profitable.

The little leather purse, which she wore beneath her clothes, was filled with silver coins. There were enough to buy a horse, and still have some left over to buy wares, when the ships came from Copenhagen. She crawled under the cart, drew out her purse, and counted the silver yet another time.

"Oh, Christ," she murmured, as she bound the leather bag and placed it again under her bodice, "protect me, and I shall give a tenth of what I have to You." Someone was approaching the cart. Quickly she whispered, "I'll give You more."

"Bodil!" a man's voice called.

She lifted the old sail just high enough to enable her to see out. It was the Commissary, who was still quite drunk.

He was smiling very smugly. He was vain enough to believe that he had made a conquest, and that Bodil loved him. He did not notice the frown on her face, as she crawled out from beneath her cart. She was, after all, only a camp follower: one of the rabble who were to be found at any fort. And was he not the Royal Supply Officer, as much above her as the King was above him? Did not the bishops say that the world was constructed with infinite wisdom? Why should he — the Commissary — find fault with it?

He opened his fist and held up a thin silver chain which had a cross dangling from it. Bodil stretched out her hand, but the man withdrew his gift. "A kiss!" he demanded.

Bodil blushed as if she were a young maiden. "Keep your gift," she replied, but not so angrily that he might be offended.

The supply officer laughed and spread the chain into a circle, by holding it in both hands. The woman bent her head before him. He placed the chain around her neck; and she did not object when he claimed his price.

"Ah, what a war!" The Commissary threw himself upon the ground and asked for some beer.

Bodil went to the cart. There was only one stoneware jug left and it was not full. She fingered the gift; the cross was light but it was of silver. As she filled Dag's tin cup, she scrutinized the supply officer. 'He is a drunkard,' she thought with disgust. 'He won't keep his commission long.' She thought of Black Lars, and wished it had been he, who had given her the cross.

As she handed the cup to the Commissary, she saw Kirsten and Dag, walking slowly towards the cart. Casually, she wondered whether the children had seen the man kiss her.

"She will be as beautiful as her mother," the Commissary remarked as he pointed at Kirsten.

Bodil's eyes followed the direction of his finger, and she noticed how thin Kirsten was and that her rags hardly covered her nakedness. "She won't be for a swine like you," she said and grinned, as though she were saying something very pleasant.

The Commissary laughed and emptied his cup. "In ten years, I shall give her a silver cross."

The children had stayed on the beach all day. Often they had gazed at the wall which enclosed the fort, but they had not talked of anything that might be going on within. But as the sun had neared the horizon, the shadow of the wall seemed to reach the cove.

"We could steal Bodil's money," Kirsten suggested.

Dag frowned, "No, I don't want to steal."

"She steals, I know she does," Kirsten replied. "To steal from a thief isn't really stealing."

Dag who was lying on his stomach drew a circle in the sand. "I don't want her money. I hate her." With both his hands he destroyed the pattern. "I don't want to be like them . . . Not any of them!" he whispered.

Kirsten drew her legs up under her body. "I hate her, too."

Dag rolled over on his back. He glanced up at the

girl and then at the sky. "I don't want to be like Peter, nor like Black Lars . . . Not even like my father." The last phrase he said in a low voice, for it gave him a strange feeling of pain. "I don't want to be like anybody I know." But then he remembered his mother. 'Maybe I would like to be like my mother,' he thought. He had dreamt of her two nights before; and when he had awakened, he had been crying.

When the beach was completely in shadows, the children rose. Silently, they walked hand in hand. In front of the door in the wall, they paused. They looked at the door. It was made of oak planks; the wind and the rain had cut deep furrows in the wood. Just as Dag was about to press his shoulder against the portal to open it, Kirsten put her hands around his neck and kissed him on the cheek.

Dag pushed her away, as he looked around quickly for fear someone might have seen them.

"But I love you," Kirsten argued.

"I don't like to be kissed," he said; then he blushed and pushed the door open.

They saw the Commissary put something around Bodil's neck and kiss her. Kirsten turned pale and knotted her hands. Dag touched her shoulder; the girl shivered and drew away from him.

CHAPTER TWENTY-FOUR

Prince Gustavus Adolphus

THE SOLDIERS RODE two by two. Steam rose from the flanks of their horses; they had ridden far that day. The soft spring earth absorbed the noise of the horses' hoofs; and in the white night, they looked like a ghost army. They had been ordered to be as quiet as they could and talking was forbidden. There were two hundred well-armed horsemen and they were dressed alike, which was uncommon for any army. Their leader, who rode in front, was followed by two officers; behind them came the standard bearer and the trumpeter.

The face of the commanding officer was so young that it was beardless. His clothes were splendid and the hilt of his sword was of gold. He kept his gaze ahead, as though he were riding alone; not even when one of the horsemen cursed because his horse had stumbled, did the youth turn around. Only a passing frown on the boyish face told that he had heard it.

When the trees became fewer and he had a view for the first time of Christianopolis, he held up his hand and tightened the reins of his horse. The officers rode up, one on either side of him. The officer on his right, speaking low, almost in a whisper, suggested that they ought to wait, until the infantry caught up with them, before attacking.

The young leader said nothing; then he turned towards the other officer. He was a man with less experience and was earnestly trying to read his commanding officer's face, before he ventured an opinion. "We should attack now," he finally said; and then bit his lower lip, for he was not certain that he had guessed correctly.

The commanding officer smiled. His smile had too much knowledge in it, to be pleasant on a face so young. He loosened his reins and touched his horse with his silver spurs, to let the animal know that he wished to gallop. The officers exchanged glances, and followed their leader: the sixteen-year-old Crown Prince of Sweden, Gustavus Adolphus.

It was near midnight, but Jens Bjornson could not sleep. He rose and dressed himself. Still buckling the belt from which his sword hung, he walked outside. The air smelled of early summer and the Commandant breathed deeply. Directly in front of his house there was no one, but he knew that he needed only to turn around, to see the revelry taking place near the wall. The greater part of his men were there, feasting with the camp followers, as they had been the night before. The Commandant loathed the camp followers; but they were as much a part of the life in his fort, as were the

cannons and the banners. He himself drank only a glass
of wine with his dinner and found drunkeness con-
temptible. 'I ought to have forbidden drinking,' he
thought; and again he resolved that he would stop
these "ridiculous festivities." Yet he did not even turn
around, for as he made the decision, there appeared in
his mind a glimpse of a grinning face.

He walked down the street towards the gate. In spite
of his instructions, he feared that the drawbridge might
not be up. He was still several yards away from it, when
he noted that there were no men posted anywhere, and
that his suspicions had been well founded.

Jens Bjornson walked across the drawbridge and
glanced up at the bastions. Four cannons pointed silently
towards the road which led to the fort. The Commandant wondered when they had last been cleaned.
'If only I had a few real soldiers,' he thought, not realizing that any man under his command would not be
an effective soldier long; for the worth of an officer can
best be measured by the discipline he keeps in times of
peace.

As he made his way back across the bridge, he heard
noise coming from the guard room: singing and laughter. 'They are probably drunk,' he thought.

For a long time he waited outside the door; only one
man was singing, but at the end of each verse all of the
men joined him:

> *Hey for the wind! And hey for the cold!*
> *God save a poor man when he grows old.*

At that very moment, when the last verse had been sung, Jens Bjornson flung open the door. What he expected to gain by this, he did not know; but certainly the banging of the door against the wall made everyone in the room aware that he was entering.

There were ten men seated on benches around a table, on which there stood several bottles of Frankish wine, which the Commandant knew must have been stolen from the King's private supplies.

All the men except one jumped to their feet. The man who remained seated was the Sergeant-at-Arms.

"I ordered the drawbridge not be lowered unless I commanded it," Jens Bjornson shouted at the Sergeant.

This gentleman smiled mockingly and said, "The Pastor last Sunday commanded everyone to behave as a true Christian; but no one here knows how a true Christian behaves."

Some of the soldiers sniggered, and the Commandant's hand touched the hilt of his sword.

"Your Excellency," began one of the older men. "One of the ropes is broken. We cannot hoist the drawbridge; but I have ordered new ropes to be put in. It will be done in the morning."

Although Jens Bjornson knew that the work ought to be done immediately — and that it could readily be accomplished since a June night is not dark — he did not reprove the delay. But the wine, he must say something about the wine. Then as if inspired, he decided that he would await the coming of the ships from Copenhagen, before he did anything. He glanced ven-

omously at the Sergeant, upon whom such scowls made
no impression. As he stepped out into the cool night
air, he thought, 'I shall have him hanged as an example,
when the reinforcements arrive.'

Jens Bjornson was standing on the drawbridge, in-
specting it once more, when he heard the hoofbeats. He
stared at the road. 'Could some of my men be returning
from Kalmar, already?' he thought.

When the soldiers came into view, and the Commandant recognized the banner that the standard bearer was
carrying, he did not curse the broken rope of the drawbridge nor the drunken soldiers; but laughed and drew
his sword. "To arms! To arms!" he cried and made a
swirling movement with it, as though he were fencing
with the night air.

The men in the guard room heard the shout and
came tumbling forth; but one glance at the advancing
horsemen sent them running down the street, a great deal
faster than they had ever run before. The Commandant
smiled broadly, when he saw them flee, with the Sergeant-at-Arms leading them; for he believed their cow-
ardice was a setting to enhance his courage. 'I shall hold
the gate alone,' he thought; then he said out loud, "I am
not afraid to die."

Later, most of the Swedes would tell that the drawbridge had been down and the gate unguarded. Only
the Prince, who gave Jens Bjornson his first wound, and
the young officer whose sword almost severed the Com-

mandant's head from his body, saw him. The other horsemen did not even notice the dead body, as they advanced to take possession of Christianopolis. Several hours afterward, the mangled corpse was discovered by a Swedish soldier, who claimed the Commandant's sword as a trophy. He had difficulty in wresting it from his hand; Jens Bjornson had so loved his sword in life that even in death he was loath to give it up.

The Swedes had galloped over the drawbridge and through the gate; now as they entered the main street of the fort they slowed down to a canter. The young Prince turned in his saddle, and shouted as loud as he could: "Let no Dane go hungry from our feast, complaining that he has not tasted our steel!"

The wild shouts of his men echoed through the streets, telling that they had understood their commander. The Prince smiled and swung his sword. "Play some music for our dance!" he called to the trumpeter.

CHAPTER TWENTY-FIVE

The Massacre of Christianopolis

THE TWO CHILDREN were lying under the cart. Kirsten was breathing deeply; she was asleep. Although it was past midnight Dag was still awake, thinking about what he ought to do, now that Peter Gram was gone. He felt as if he were lost in a labyrinth, like the passages in the dungeon of the castle at Elsinore, that his mother had told him about, from which only dreams offer an escape.

He lifted the old sail and looked up at the sky; it was cloudless and in the east a pink tinge was visible. He glanced at Kirsten; and at that moment, she smiled in her sleep. Quietly, he crawled outside. When he let the canvas fall back into place, he listened to hear if he might have awakened her.

The scene near the wall looked almost the same as it had the night before, but the revelers were not as noisy or as gay; a kind of desperation seemed to have overtaken them. No one noticed Dag; and he, not wishing to be seen, walked quickly towards the wharf.

The gate was open, which was not unusual, for no one

expected an attack from the sea. A slight breeze was blowing from land. The crews were on board the three small sailing ships, getting the vessels ready for departure. Dag asked one of the sailors where they were going.

"To Kalmar!" he replied and spat into the sea.

Dag considered asking if he might be allowed to go with them; but then he decided that it was not worth the trouble, for certainly he would be refused.

He walked to the end of the wharf and looked towards that point on the mainland where he had last seen Peter Gram. 'If only I were fourteen,' he thought, 'then I could be a drummer.' He clenched his fists. He was not fourteen. He was a child caught in a world which had no place for a child.

While he gazed at the stones of the wharf, he suddenly saw his situation very clearly: Black Lars and Peter had gone, but Bodil had not sent him away, and in Kirsten he had a friend. He would stay with Bodil until he was twelve or thirteen. The very act of having made up his mind to dismiss thoughts of flight made Dag hopeful. Even thinking about Bodil's beatings — and she did beat the children cruelly when the world was against her — did not seem as unbearable, as dreams that could not be realized.

'I could not live in the forest alone,' he thought. Noticing a pebble, he picked it up and walked to the edge of the wharf to drop it into the water.

"The King," he murmured, remembering his other dream. He watched the rings grow large and disappear, becoming part of the ripples which the light breeze

caused on the sea. "Even if the King had known what
had happened to·my mother and father, he wouldn't
have cared." The world at once became ever so large
and ever so small.

Suddenly a fish leapt into the air. Dag bent down to
get a better view of the water below the surface. 'A
bigger fish must have been chasing it, and it was trying
to escape,' he thought.

The noise of the horses galloping across the drawbridge could be heard throughout the fort. Dag wondered what it might be: a carriage sounded differently,
so did carts and wagons. Could the Scots officer and
his men — and Black Lars! — be returning from Kalmar? But then he heard the blare of the trumpet and
he started to run back towards the fort.

As he approached the gate in the wall, he stopped;
the Sergeant-at-Arms, waving wildly, was just coming
through it. Behind him came the soldiers, and the expressions of terror on their faces told that some calamity
had happened.

"Pull up the sails! Pull up the sails!" the Sergeant
screamed; as he looked desperately from one·to the
other of the three vessels, trying to guess which one was
most easily gotten underway.

"We are not sailing before sunrise," one of the sailors
replied, lazily.

"You will never live to see it!" the Sergeant hissed,
as he leapt onto the nearest of the ships.

A few shots were heard and then someone screamed:
not in pain nor in fear, but in death. That cry was like

a command to the sailors; on all three ships everyone started working at once.

Before the moorings could be cast, the boats were overloaded. The protests of the seamen meant nothing, to those who realized that the sea was the only road of escape. Dag just managed to get through the gate, when he was met by another stream of fleeing people. Had he fallen, that river of frightened human beings would have been no more merciful than the great rivers are, when they swell with water in spring.

In the street he saw the first dead body. He recognized the lifeless form as an old soldier whom he had spoken with the day before. The portal of the church was closed and there was no one in the square, except for the dead. As if it were some duty that he was bound to perform, Dag went from one corpse to the other. At the far end of the square he saw the body of a boy, younger than himself, with a gaping wound in his neck. Dag looked up at the sky, which was turning a light blue as morning approached. Aloud he said, "But he was only a child." He had spoken slowly, as if this were a riddle he wanted to find the answer to.

Three soldiers came riding out of one of the streets; their horses were trotting and they were laughing. In front of them ran a fat woman. Her face was covered with sweat and she was heaving for breath. Every time she slackened, the soldiers pricked her with their swords. Finally, she fell and the horses leapt over her.

Dag did not wait to see what else happened to the

woman. He fled down the street without turning back.

"Kirsten . . . Kirsten . . ." Dag heard himself call-
ing the girl's name, as he passed the Commandant's house.
In every direction he saw Swedish soldiers. Some of
them had dismounted, in order to search for loot.

"Kirsten!" he cried and he ran towards the cart,
certain that he would find her dead body there.

In front of the cart lay Bodil. She was dead. Her
bodice had been torn and her little bag of silver was
gone. One of the soldiers, who was rummaging among
her things, noticed the boy; and gesturing with his head
towards the corpse of the woman, he asked, "Was she
your mother?"

"Yes," Dag lied.

The soldier smiled at him; it was a strange smile, like
the one you often see on the faces of children just before they start to cry.

"Dag!"

The boy heard Kirsten's voice, and turned to see her
running towards him.

"Kirsten!" he cried and ran to meet her.

The children embraced and said each other's names
over and over again.

"I've found a hiding place," she whispered. "There's
a shed behind the Commandant's house."

At that moment Prince Gustavus Adolphus came
riding onto the field. With him was the older officer,
and following them was a group of soldiers. Among
these was a very young lad — he was but sixteen. His
sword was drawn, but he had found no opportunity for

using it and the blade was clean. Being neither boy nor
man, he blushed easily and had no beard to hide behind.
He was only a fool but at that age when fools are most
dangerous.

One of his comrades, who was riding abreast of him,
made some jesting remark about the virginlike appear-
ance of his sword, as if its unbloodied state were a
shame which reflected upon its master. The youth's
face grew red and he looked about the field to find an
enemy. He saw the two children; and swinging his
sword in the same manner as the Prince had, when he
led the charge on Christianopolis, the young man
spurred his horse into a gallop.

Dag heard the hoofbeats and turned only to see that
no escape was possible. He pushed Kirsten to the ground
and would have thrown himself on top of her, but
for Dag the world grew dark. A heart was still that
had proved it could beat for love, and so be worthy
to live within the body of a man.

The youth who had shed a child's blood to hide a
blush, checked his horse and circled his crime. He
saw the girl cast herself upon the body of the boy; and
suddenly he remembered that he had a sister at home.

The Prince, who had been watching the spectacle, had
cried out, when he realized what the young soldier was
about to do. But that madness, which every man who
has taken part in war knows and fears, had taken possession of the Swedish soldiers. Man is half sheep and half
wolf; and sheep can be commanded by a shepherd but
wolves cannot. Their weariness and the first shedding

of unnecessary blood had worked upon these men, as wine does upon a starving man.

The order for the massacre had been his, but now as a spectator the Prince became angry. With raised sword, he advanced towards the youth. The lad, who worshipped his Prince, gazed at him and then looked down at his own bloody sword. Suddenly he realized how foolish he had been; and he wanted to cry out that he was sorry; but the Prince's sword pierced his heart and he fell from his horse without a murmur.

The face of Prince Gustavus Adolphus was pale. He turned to the officer, who had ridden up beside him, and whispered, "I have been a fool." But it was said more to himself than to anyone else.

The officer smiled. He had been through many battles and seen many horrible sights.

"Magnus!" The Prince's face was still a boy's, but his voice was not. "If I cannot command my arm then it shall be cut off. How shall I lead armies if I cannot command myself?"

Shaking his head, the man whom the Prince had called Magnus looked intently at the arm that was outstretched in front of him. "Your Highness is young."

The Prince slowly lowered his arm and smiled sourly. He wiped the sword on the hide of his horse, before he returned it to its sheath. Finally, he noticed Kirsten, who was crying and talking to Dag as if he were alive. He took a gold coin from his purse and threw it in her direction. It fell near Dag's feet and the girl did not even see it.

Prince Gustavus Adolphus spurred his horse and rode towards the Commandant's house; his officers and his men followed him. But one of the riders turned back. He wanted the gold coin, not for its value but because it had belonged to the Prince.

EPILOGUE

FOUR MONTHS have passed since the King died. I
am no longer living in Frederiks Castle, and when I
walk by the sentries at the gate, they do not notice me.
The wheel of fortune is forever turning and only the
fool thinks it will stop for him.

The ceilings of my rooms are low; in order to enter
my house you would have to bend your head. Yet my
garden is a pleasant place. Beneath the cherry tree
there is a wooden bench, where I like to sit, when the sun
shines and God is smiling to the world. From that
garden seat I travel, riding that swift horse called
memory, back into the lost kingdom of my life.

I have described the fall of Christianopolis and told
of Dag's death, yet the story is not finished. I must tell,
too, what happened to the survivors. The three little
boats were caught by heavy winds in Kalmar Sound
and all on board were lost, which proves that those
who are meant to be drowned are never hanged.

Black Lars died in Germany, that year when the
plague reaped so great a harvest, that the war almost

stopped for lack of hands to wield swords. His daughter is married to a farmer who has land near the old Cloister at Esrum. I met one of her children the other day in the square; he is a handsome youth, who reminded me of his grandfather.

What happened to Kirsten? Again I see her, as I met her in the clearing in the woods not far from Christianopolis. For my name is Peter Gram. I was that youth who ran away.

She was seated in the grass, near the road; her head was bowed. She did not see me before I called her name. "Where is Dag?" I asked and looked around, hoping to see the boy.

Kirsten smiled. "He is dead. They all are dead." She folded her hands as if she were about to pray.

What I vowed to do for Dag, I did for Kirsten. I found a family who would take her in; and I paid for her upbringing as if she were my sister. But the soul can be wounded as well as the body. She grew up to be a quiet woman who seldom smiled and never laughed; and yet children are fond of her. I thought she would never marry, but she finally did. Her husband is a potter by trade and almost as silent as she. They have several children. I am godfather to the oldest, a boy who is named Dag. Her husband is a master of his craft and they have fared well. They live in Elsinore.

I shall not end this story from my youth in the fashion of the day, by spelling out a moral that can be learned from it. For the untold tale is an immoral story, a shameful tale of how I committed treason to my own heart. Oh you captains and commanders of men, dismount from your proud horses and walk the battlefields; do not count the dead but look at them; and then, if you dare, claim your victories.

I am old. My life is done. May Christ judge me with mercy. May you, who have read these pages, bear good fortune with ease and meet adversity with courage.

Near Frederiks Castle,
the thirtieth day of June,
1648 years after the birth
of Our Blessed Saviour.

I wish to express my gratitude to Denmark's National Bank who through their Jubilee Fund made it possible for me to do the necessary research for writing *The Untold Tale*. I am not only indebted to them for their generosity but for the encouragement which their support implied.